Christmas

 at

Whitefriars

a novella

ELIZABETH
CAMDEN

CHAPTER ONE

YORKSHIRE, ENGLAND
1912

"ARE YOU SURE you want me to do this?" Nick asked as he prepared to fuse the pipe joints. "As soon as I solder this pipe in, there's no turning back. The tower will get hot water, and your washroom gets nothing. We can't heat both."

Was there anything on earth more delightful than a long, hot bath?

Mary Beckwith was thirty-one years old but had never had the joy of simply turning on a spigot to indulge in a piping hot bath. Many people probably thought growing up in an actual castle must be the epitome of luxury, but the truth was that castles were drafty, hard to renovate, and lacked the amenities 1912 had to offer. Of all the inconveniences at the Whitefriars castle, the lack of modern plumbing had always been the biggest discomfort.

Nine years ago, Whitefriars had a huge infusion of American cash to begin repairing centuries of decay. After refurbishing the roof, the first thing Mary ordered was running water and modern drainage. She got the plumbing installed, but the American money ran out before a heating system for the water could be added. Soon that would change. She sat on a padded stool from the mid-Tudor era and handed tools to her brother-in-law as he clanged a pipe connecting the hot water boiler.

Mary bit her lip. How long had she dreamed of the decadence of a long, hot bath in her own washroom? No more lugging buckets of steaming water to the clawfoot tub to make the icy water tepid. She'd hoped those days were coming to an end, but the boiler she'd purchased for Whitefriars wasn't large enough to heat the water for all the rooms. That meant the kitchen and the tower would get hot water, while she would have to wait for next year's infusion of American cash to heat her own washroom.

"Send it to the tower," she said a little reluctantly.

She could do without hot water, but the tower rooms couldn't, for rich tourists expected hot water. Their first guests would be arriving in February, and the brochure promised modern amenities.

"You're a good egg," Nick said as he pumped oil into a handheld blow torch. She wasn't exactly sure what he meant by "a good egg," but given the approval in his voice, she assumed it was an American expression for something positive. She and Nick came from different worlds. Nine years ago, her brother moved to America and married Nick's sister, a woman from a family of plumbers. Sir Colin Beckwith had lived in New York ever since, but he visited Whitefriars often, along with his wife, children, and in-laws. Nick tinkered with the castle's plumbing whenever he came, and Mary happily accepted his help updating the castle's rudimentary water system.

All over England there were estates with the same problems. Decaying roofs, massive repair bills, and crippling taxes. Heating a castle cost a fortune, and living in one often required chipping away a thin film of ice that formed in the washbasin overnight. The installation of running water, especially *hot* running water, was no easy task.

The moment Nick proclaimed the boiler ready, she raced to the kitchen, eager to try it out. She breathed a sigh of pleasure when stepping inside, for the kitchen was always the warmest room in the entire castle. There was an ancient brick fireplace on one wall of the kitchen, but after the renovation it also featured a modern cast-iron stove, a marble-topped counter for food preparation, and a white porcelain sink. She turned the spigot and listened to the hiss and bubble of water as it travelled through the copper pipes.

Nick entered a few moments later, standing in the stone archway leading to the kitchen. "You'll need to give it twenty or thirty minutes for the water to get good and hot," he cautioned. "And it will heat faster if you don't run the water."

She twisted the spigot closed. "I shall stand here in anticipation," she teased. "I've been looking forward to this moment all my life and don't mind waiting."

Colin strode into the room, his cheeks still red from the December chill, but his blond hair was as perfectly groomed as always. He'd just come from the tower to inspect the newly delivered bed frame, wardrobe, and end tables.

"I don't like the furniture you bought," he said.

Her face fell. "Why not?" She'd spent a fortune on the brass headboard with darling little filigree pineapples topping each of the spindles. It would never rot or suffer from burrowing insects.

"It's too new and shiny," he said as he grabbed the kettle to begin preparing tea. "People don't rent a castle for new things."

"I could hardly use what was in there," she defended. The tower roof had been failing for decades, bats inhabited the chimney, and white scale bloomed on the stone walls. For decades they had been using the tower to store obsolete farm equipment and broken furniture. She dragged it all outside and held a huge bonfire down by the stream to purge it all.

The three-story tower had the most potential for being transformed into a charming retreat. Its isolation from the rest of the castle gave it the privacy long-term guests would love. Rich tourists could come for between one and three months, idling in the country, taking long walks, hunting, fishing, or simply enjoying the chance to live in a real castle. The tower overlooked miles of rolling countryside and Mary personally made new curtains for all the windows. Other tasks she had to hire out, and she spent a small fortune to plaster the walls, install new tile floors, a modern washroom, and brand-new furniture.

Except now Colin found fault with the furniture she'd purchased.

"Scuff it up a little," he suggested. "Maybe a little sandpaper or a few dings with a hammer. You need to aim for that whiff of seventeenth-century charm in everything."

"The tower had the whiff of medieval black mold," she said. "I wanted everything new."

"Doesn't matter," Colin said as he took a china cup from

the shelf. "You need to scuff up the furniture or replace it with real antiques."

"Are you serious?" It was hard to tell when Colin was joking. His aristocratic formality sometimes made him seem like he'd been born wearing that starched collar. She was comfortable on the farm, even though it meant counting the number of goats born each season and digging muck out of the irrigation lines. The fact that Colin abandoned her and Whitefriars when he married and settled in America?

Well… she didn't mind. Not too much, anyway. And right now she needed his insight. Colin lived in Manhattan and mingled with the type of freshly minted millionaires she would depend on to make a go of this renovation. He understood them far better than she.

"I'm serious," he said. "Why do you think the Wootens wanted to partner with us to begin with? It wasn't for my good looks."

The Wootens were the American family who paid them a fortune to license the Whitefriars name and image. All over the world, millions of people bought overpriced jars of jam, sauces, and baked goods that carried an engraving of the Whitefriars castle on the label. It lent immediate prestige to a mass-produced product, and the Wootens paid well for it. She'd never met old Mr. Wooten or his son, but she'd played along with the illusion that the American products had some sort of affiliation with the estate. No one ever looked too closely, for which she was grateful. She gladly cashed the licensing fees and applied the revenue toward the never-ending checklist of improvements for the castle.

"Let's go to the tower and you can tell me what I should have bought," Mary said, trying to mask the stress in her voice.

The furniture was bought and paid for, and it seemed odd to deliberately damage it, but Colin understood rich Americans better than she. They left the untouched tea cooling on the table as they crossed through the great hall and down the east wing toward the tower.

She loved this walk. This part of the castle dated to 1388, the same year *The Canterbury Tales* had been written. The stone floors had been polished smooth by five centuries of foot traffic, and she liked to imagine the countless generations of Beckwiths before her. Those people survived the War of the Roses and lived through the crucible of Cromwell and the civil wars.

Colin stopped her in the middle of the great hall. "Why is the post stacking up on the front table?"

A glance at the table in the entryway showed the last four deliveries from New York, gathering dust while Mary had been getting the house up to snuff for the Christmas holidays. Colin brought his wife Lucy and their two toddlers, along with Lucy's brother and his family. She was proud of the progress she'd made at Whitefriars and wanted them to see it at its best, leaving her no time to review the dreary paperwork from New York.

"It's nothing," she replied. "Everett Wooten bombards me with the financial reports every week. I don't know why he bothers. A quarterly report would be fine."

Colin paused. "Are you sure? There's quite a stack here."

He wandered to the hall table, his footsteps echoing on the stone tiles. The great hall hadn't needed much modification. The ceiling soared high and was covered by the original hand-hewn timbers that lent a warm, gothic appeal to the space. Each end of the great hall had an immense fireplace, though they rarely used them except on formal occasions.

Colin's expression turned into a frown as he flipped through the stacks of accumulated letters. She tried to hide her impatience, for time was growing short if she was to make major alterations in the tower before February. The weekly reports from America were always so routine and she had more important things to do than jump when they arrived.

"I refuse to get swept up into the whirlwind of Everett's insanity," she said. "I wrote him long ago that I pay little attention to his weekly sales statistics."

She had nine years of correspondence with Everett Wooten, the son of the company's owner. They got along smashingly well, even though they'd never met. While he was easy to deal with on paper, she sensed he might be unendurable in person, for his pedantic nature rang through his letters like the clarion blast of a trumpet. She once asked him why he insisted on sending weekly reports since he knew she rarely read them.

Complacency breeds failure, he wrote back in reply. *Weekly reports are a company's lifeblood.*

As frustrating as his nitpicky ways were, she couldn't complain about how helpful he'd been over the years. In truth, she'd leaned on him too much in keeping Whitefriars afloat. When their wheat fields suffered from waterlogged soil, he recommended a drainage technique that could easily be implemented. When she worried about falling grain prices, he recommended foreign markets where she'd get a better price.

"Truly, there's no need to review the reports," she said. "While I'm glad Everett's products are selling well, I can't be bothered with a blizzard of paperwork."

"*Are* the products selling well?"

She shrugged. "I assume so. It seems like he's always on a quest to bombard another market or saturate the world with Whitefriars labels." The British army could learn a thing or two about world domination from the systematic way Everett planned his campaigns.

She turned curious eyes to Colin. "You've met him. What do you think of him?" Mary had never travelled farther than London, so Colin handled all the face-to-face interaction with the Wootens.

"He's an odd one," Colin finally said.

"What does 'an odd one' mean?"

"He's very formal, all business, no chitchat. Ever," Colin replied. "He has an obsessive need to control things. But he's got his quirks, and they're odd."

"Such as?"

Colin set the envelopes back on the table. "Rumor has it that he has peculiar food preferences. On any given day, Everett Wooten eats only one color. Green, for example. He'll eat only green vegetables, green apples, lime sherbet, spinach soup, that sort of thing. Then a day of yellow food, then orange food."

She stifled a laugh. "How does one eat only orange food?"

Colin shrugged. "I have no idea. He's got five or six colors, and he eats them in the exact same order, week in, week out. Or at least… that's the rumor. Having met him, it wouldn't surprise me. Look, are you certain those envelopes are of no concern? Everett Wooten is not a person you want to alienate."

"Trust me, they are only boring weekly revenue reports. If you need help falling asleep tonight, you have my blessing to take them upstairs and read to your heart's content. They are more effective than any sleeping tonic."

She led the way out of the great hall and down a long corridor toward the tower. They passed numerous locked doors, for most of the rooms hadn't yet been renovated. The barren, stone rooms were a little depressing, but slowly she was finding the money to renovate more and more of the castle. For now, the long corridor and the locked rooms had an unexpected benefit of creating a sense of privacy for the guests who would soon be staying in the tower.

She unlocked the heavy oak door and lifted the latch, pleased at how easily it glided open without the hint of a squeak. Removing the rust and oiling the hinges had been done with her own two hands, and she was proud of it. She stepped inside, breathing deeply of the scent of lemon wax on the newly restored wooden window casements.

She watched Colin's face as he scanned the ground-floor room. Surely he couldn't find fault in the entry room, could he? In addition to the restored floors, the room had been re-plastered and painted, but the old diamond-paned windows were still the same. Some of their best antique furniture had been used to create a cozy sitting area in this ground room of the three-story tower.

"Good work on the tapestries," Colin said approvingly, for they were also originals she managed to salvage through a painstaking process of cleaning and restoration. It might have been easier to buy new, but these originally came from a convent in Spain. They'd been brought home by an ancestor who'd rescued them from a fire during the Peninsular War. How could she let them go because of a little moth damage? During long winter nights she'd carefully stitched the threadbare patches, then reinforced the back of the tapestry with cotton supports. Now they warmed the otherwise cold and echoey room.

Colin wiggled the edge of the tapestry. "This is the kind of feeling you need to aim for. Old, but clean. I can see a little wear along the edges, but people will forgive you that."

"If they want old, I should have kept the hot water for myself and put a slop bucket and washbasin in here."

Colin flashed her a wink. "All bets are off when it comes to plumbing. They'll want the best when it comes to that."

He headed over to the newly constructed washroom on the main floor. It was her greatest achievement. An interior wall of matching plaster created a private room that had a toilet, washstand, and an actual shower. A shower!

"Shall we test the hot water?" she asked. "Nick says it should be warm by now."

She held her breath as she turned the spigot. It took a moment of gurgling and hissing before a blast of icy water came forth. She almost pulled her fingers away, but after a moment the water warmed, then grew hot.

"Hot water!" she cried out and impulsively hugged Colin. He laughed, even though he enjoyed hot water all the time in his fancy Manhattan apartment. Oh, how she was going to love this! She would come over and take a hot shower this very night.

A winding staircase curved around the interior of the tower and took them to the second floor with its additional parlor and an eating area. The top floor had two compact bedrooms and a spectacular view of the entire estate, nine hundred rolling acres of farmland, meadows, and forests. With no leaves on the trees it was easy to see the silvery stream snaking through the property. Perfect for fishing. Her brochure boasted of the hiking, hunting, and fishing available at Whitefriars. It was about the only entertainment she could offer, for they were an hour from the attractions in the city of York.

Colin tapped the shiny brass bedpost with his fingernails, making a pinging sound. "This is what the tourists don't want," he said. "It looks brand new, like it just came from Harrods."

That was because it did. She lifted her chin, trying not to be hurt by the look of distaste on Colin's face. Did he have any idea how hard she'd been slaving away over this castle while he lived in the lap of luxury in Manhattan? Couldn't he at least say the bedroom looked nice? Its view of the countryside was possibly the best in all of Yorkshire. There wasn't a trace of mold or a speck of limescale. She would love to stay in a room this fresh and pretty, and all Colin could do was gripe about the brass bed.

Well. She wouldn't let it annoy her. She looked forward to these two-week Christmas reunions all year. Tonight they would have a feast, full of laughter and conversation. It wasn't as if she hadn't known her brother was a fussy stickler for detail.

"Are you sure you shouldn't go check those letters from Wooten?" Colin asked as he peered out the top window. "They could be important."

"Very well, let's go." The sooner they could dispose of those weekly reports, the sooner she could get down to planning the evening's dinner.

***

They weren't weekly reports.

Colin wanted to take them back to the library to give them a good look, and he waited until he was seated at the immense desk to open them. Mary watched the color drain from Colin's face as he read the first page from the stack of papers he pulled from the envelope.

"We're being sued," he said.

"What?" she screeched.

"Everett says we've broken our terms of the contract. He's exercising his right to repossess Whitefriars."

The words were a slap in the face. Colin had signed a mountain of contracts when the deal with the Wootens had first been struck nine years ago. The contracts had been through an army of attorneys for both sides, but their only real obligation was to preserve the external appearance and reputation of the castle.

Mary raced to find the original contract to see the terms Everett claimed they violated. Colin looked badly shaken as he tore open the other envelopes, laying all the pages out in order across the surface of the table.

Apparently, Everett Wooten had been trying to get her attention for some time. Even now he was in the nearby city of York, waiting for her to call on him in person to discuss remedies.

Remedies? This was her home. Her lifeblood was in this castle. Over the past decade she'd given everything to rescuing this magnificent wreck of a castle from the ravages of time, mold, swamp, and decay.

Mary collapsed into a chair, unable to even speak. Over the next few minutes, Lucy, Nick, and his wife gathered in the room, stunned at this horrible turn of events. Nick's wife advised her to lay on the sofa and elevate her feet. Rosalind was a doctor, but not *that* kind of doctor. A specialist in water-borne viruses, how could Rosalind help with a broken heart? Whitefriars was her heart, her soul, and everything else that mattered to her. Seventy tenants lived on this land, and some millionaire from New York City thought he could waltz in and take over?

Colin and his wife both paged through the stack of documents Everett Wooten sent, reading quickly as Mary's world collapsed around her.

"I think this is the problem," Lucy said, pulling a small item clipped from the newspaper out of the stack. It was the announcement Mary placed in the *New York Times*, advertising the availability of Whitefriars to lease. She did not misrepresent the castle. She described the amenities of the tower rooms and the nine hundred acres suitable for hunting, fishing, or invigorating walks in the fresh country air. And surely Everett couldn't object to the image on the advertisement, for it was the same one he used on all the Whitefriars branded products of which he was so proud. The image was of the castle, set in an oval frame with a few trees and rolling hills in the background. It was a lovely image, and now world-famous thanks to the licensing agreement they signed with the Wootens.

"What's wrong with the advertisement?" she asked, mortified how badly her voice trembled.

"He might not like that you're leasing the castle," Lucy said. "It might seem a little lowbrow in his eyes."

She raised her chin. "Our title dates to the seventeenth century. We have hosted kings and princes. Everett Wooten's father started life as a shoe polish salesman."

"Pipe down there, ma'am," Nick said, a hint of warning in his voice. Maybe she sounded snobbish, but there was nothing lowbrow about Whitefriars, even though she'd spent most of her adult life rescuing it from decaying roofs and waterlogged fields.

"He states in his letter that any material change to the external appearance or reputation of Whitefriars will allow him to exercise his right to buy out the property." Colin swallowed hard. "And since the Wootens have already contributed three million dollars toward the renovations, we own less than twenty percent equity in the estate."

"Twenty percent? That can't be right."

It was. As Colin explained, the deal he negotiated all those years ago awarded the Wootens substantial equity in return for the massive infusion of cash to salvage a castle. The deal allowed Mary and her heirs the right to occupy the house in perpetuity, but most of the equity now belonged to the Wootens.

She couldn't resent Colin for the deal. At the time he signed the contract, the castle was on the verge of becoming uninhabitable. Colin's deal both saved the castle and let her live in it forever. He knew what Whitefriars meant to her, and how she'd be devasted to be driven off the estate.

"We need to move quickly," Colin said. "Everett has been in town all week. He's staying at the Knightsbridge Inn. If we leave now, we can possibly see him this evening."

Her apprehension ratcheted higher. She'd visited York in the past, but it never went well, and over the years her anxiety about the city had grown worse. York had once been a charming small city, but in recent years it had become the hub for dozens of railways and all their associated ruckus.

Confectionery factories and woolen mills further diversified the economy, but the crowds, the smoke, and the noise made it difficult for her. She would happily live out her days in rural isolation if it meant she never had to set foot in a city again.

She pretended not to understand Colin's meaning as she stood. "Let's hurry, then. I'll fetch your coat and put these papers into order for your meeting."

"Mary, you need to be there."

She turned to face him, praying he would understand. "I don't know much about business. I think you'd be far better at negotiating a way out of this mess."

"Mary, you need to be there," Colin repeated calmly.

She closed her eyes. Leasing the tower had been her idea. She was obviously the right person to go, but these attacks of panic could come out of nowhere, and one was hovering right now, threatening to choke off her breath.

"I'll be with you the entire time," Colin said, his voice kind and reassuring. "After coming so far, I won't let you falter, but we have to play this wisely." The corners of his mouth turned down as he eyed the six envelopes she'd let stack up. Her carelessness had already put them on the wrong footing with Everett, and she wouldn't exacerbate it by hiding here like a coward.

But this was going to be hard. She hadn't travelled farther than the local village in more than two years, and York was such an industrialized blight on the countryside. It now had ninety thousand people crammed into a few square miles. The noise, the congestion, the towering smokestacks and crowded streets. No, she couldn't do it. Even now a wave of dizziness threatened, and she braced a hand against the wall to steady herself.

Right over an old musket hole in the limestone wall. Legend had it that the lady of the manor fired that musket when the officers from the king came to arrest her husband for owning an illegal printing press. It was a hanging offence, and her valor gave the husband enough time to disassemble and hide the press. He lived to be an old man thanks to the courage of his wife that day.

Mary drew a steadying breath. She would be worthy of her ancestors. Over the centuries this castle had witnessed epic battles, survived floods and famine, served as a hospital during outbreaks of disease, celebrated feasts after victories, and led the people during times of mourning. She would not be worthy of Whitefriars if she couldn't leave its walls to fight for it.

She squared her shoulders and faced Colin. "Let me fetch my cloak, and we can leave immediately."

CHAPTER TWO

IT TOOK ALMOST an hour for the carriage to make it into York. Whitefriars had once been a monastery, and its location chosen for its isolation. Getting into town was a bit of a challenge, and Mary clasped the leather hand strap as the carriage bumped and jostled along pitted country roads.

"Tell me everything about Everett Wooten," she said, determined to handle this meeting with aplomb, for Whitefriars depended on it.

"He's a hard man to get to know," Colin said. "Our meetings have always been brief. Very businesslike. He knows exactly what he wants, and we usually come to an agreement quickly. I've gotten along okay with him, but he's not afraid to lock horns with people. Last summer there was a revolt at one of the canning factories. He wanted to start operating the facility around the clock, and the workers objected, even after he offered a higher wage to people on the night shift. When they still objected, he took the overnight shift for a solid month, just to show them it could be done."

She lifted her brows in surprise. "He worked on the cannery floor? Like a common factory worker?"

"He did. And in the end, he got his way. That factory now operates around the clock, seven days a week."

She'd always known Everett was a competitive businessman. Their correspondence proved that, although he'd always been generous with his advice to her, despite being a little formal and scary.

"But what is he *like*?" she pressed. "His personality? His likes and dislikes?"

Colin shrugged. "That's all I really know. He doesn't engage in idle chatter. I never see him at society events. I once invited him to a golf outing, but he turned it down. Same with a fishing trip. He simply has no discernable interests outside of business."

None of this sounded very promising. She had to find some way to establish a common bond before they got down to brass tacks.

"Does he have a wife? Children?"

Colin frowned. "There was a bit of a scandal a few years back. He was engaged to a woman from upstate. The church had been reserved, hall rented, flowers ordered, the whole works. He called it off a week ahead of the ceremony and it caused a big uproar. The girl's father threatened a lawsuit and would have won, for the girl was the wronged party. Wooten settled out of court. No one ever learned the cause of the debacle. Look, he's a bit of a stick in the mud, but we don't need to be friends to do business with him. All we need to do is smooth his ruffled feathers and hopefully this whole thing will blow over."

She drew a steadying breath, dreading this meeting.

Dreading it *all*… the city, the stress, the unknown. The carriage slowed as traffic snarled the streets. The lampposts were decorated with Christmas wreaths and bow-fronted shop windows draped with red ribbons, but none of the season's cheer could penetrate the hard wall of anxiety that encased her spirit.

They had arrived at the Knightsbridge. It was the city's finest inn, with liveried footmen standing on the marble portico and gaslight torches flickering in the darkness.

"I'll meet you in the front lobby," Colin said. "The meeting may run long, and I want to tip the men at the stable to give the horses a rub down."

She nodded tightly, the frosty air penetrating her cloak as she disembarked. The chill prompted her to hurry up the steps, and one of the footmen opened the door for her. She nodded her thanks but was too nervous to speak. Cities always did this to her.

Still, she couldn't help a little smile at how nicely the hotel lobby looked, already fully decked out for Christmas. Garlands of pine boughs wrapped around the marble columns at the front counter. A Christmas tree in the sitting area filled the lobby with the scent of pine.

Her footsteps were muffled by thick carpets as she approached the front desk, but she couldn't ask after Mr. Wooten. It would be the kiss of death for an unmarried woman to inquire after the whereabouts of a male guest. Everett wasn't even expecting them. For all she knew, he'd become disgusted by her lack of response and had already left for America. She wished Colin was here, and that her heart wasn't pounding so hard. She was beginning to perspire, and it was hard to breathe.

Oh please, not now. These attacks of panic had plagued her ever since she was a girl. Sometimes they were brought on by city noise, sometimes for no reason whatsoever. All she knew was that a sense of doom was closing in around her, making it hard to breathe. She couldn't collapse. She would will the panic away.

Barely able to breathe, she approached the front counter, cutting ahead of a line of gentlemen to get the attention of the only clerk.

"Please… can I have a glass of water?"

The clerk must have noticed her distress, for he dropped the card he was about to file. "Right away, madam."

She braced her hands on the cool marble of the counter, leaning her weight on it lest she faint. Breathe in and breathe out. She could do this.

Except now her hands had gone numb. The clerk returned with a cup of water, setting it on the counter, but she couldn't even lift her hand to take it. She heard voices, but they all sounded as if they were coming from far away. If only Colin would come get her. They could board the carriage and go home and she could collapse in the privacy of Whitefriars.

"Shall I send for someone?" the clerk asked, but all she could do was shake her head.

Someone put his hand on her shoulder. "You'll be all right, ma'am," a calm voice said. The man was tall, but that was all she could sense, for she didn't trust herself to lift her hands from the counter to look at him. She'd probably topple over.

"Follow me," the man said. "I know what to do."

A gloved hand lifted her palm off the counter, encasing her hand as he guided her to the far side of the lobby. What a fine leather glove he wore. It was an inane thought… to admire a man's gloves at a time like this… but she followed him and soon they were behind the Christmas tree, a padded bench at her side.

"Have a seat," the man said.

She couldn't. She might tip over if she tried.

"Sit," he ordered, turning her shoulders so that she was aligned with the bench. It hit her behind the knees and she plopped onto it. He joined her and, oddly, upended the sack he carried, dumping an array of candy and wrapped bakery goods onto the carpet. He crunched the paper bag and squeezed the top.

"Hold this to your face," he said.

She reared back, looking at him in shock. He had light brown hair and fine blue eyes and a stern mouth, but his face seemed kind.

"Trust me on this," he said. "Our cook had the same disorder as you seem to have. Use this paper bag to get control of your breathing. It will help."

She still didn't understand, but he pressed the bag to her face, its dry paper rasping against her skin. It still smelled like peppermint candies.

His hand was on her back, rubbing gently. She ought to haul off and slap him… the impudence… but this bag, the sensation, the easing of the panic, the scent of peppermints…

"You're doing well. Keep it up."

How could something as silly as a paper bag provide such relief? Her parents had taken her to a dozen doctors. Written to specialists in Berlin and Paris. None of it helped, but this paper bag, it was amazing. She lowered it to ask how he knew of such a trick.

He immediately lifted it again, pressing it to her face. "Don't give up too quickly," he said. "We'll just sit here for a while. We don't have a care in the world."

Easy for him to say. He wasn't collapsing into a puddle of nerves and about to have his house yanked out from under him. "I feel like a fool," she said, her voice muffled through the paper bag. He leaned over to pluck a piece of candy from the carpet, slowly freeing it from the paper wrapping.

"Taffy drop?" he asked her politely, but she shook her head. He popped the candy into his mouth, chewing slowly as he gazed toward the front of the lobby as though lost in thought. How cool he seemed, as though he was totally absorbed as he analyzed the taste of the chewy glob.

So much candy still lay spilled on the floor, but he seemed disinterested as he sat beside her. What an oddly heroic move to casually dump it all out to let her use of the sack. The candy came from the Rowan Confectionery, one of the best in the city. He must have quite a sweet tooth, because he'd bought hard candies, chews, and a dozen pastries, all safely wrapped in paper branded with the Rowan Confectionery.

"Good?" she asked after he finished chewing, but it took him a while to answer.

"Not really. Too much sugar. It overpowers the natural apricot flavoring."

He must be affiliated with one of the dozens of confectioneries that had sprung up in York. It was one of the reasons the city had grown so quickly, for thousands of people flooded the city to find work in the various candy and chocolate factories.

She pulled the bag a few inches away. "Are you in the candy business?" she asked, then quickly covered her nose again. Nothing in her life had ever curbed her fits of panic as effectively as this paper bag, and she didn't care if she looked silly. It worked.

"Not yet," he said. "Possibly soon."

He went back to staring straight ahead and the discussion was at an end. She couldn't carry it because of the bag, and he didn't seem interested in holding up his end of the conversation. So they sat. At least the Christmas tree partially screened her from the bustle of the lobby.

At last she saw Colin striding forward, scanning the crowd for her.

"Colin!" she called out, raising her hand. He spotted her and walked over. She was about to explain the bag, but he wasn't even looking at her, he looked only at her companion.

"Everett," he said to the man, holding out his hand. "I see you've met Mary."

The man rose and returned his handshake. "Colin. Good to see you."

Oh, good heavens! The man spoke with an American accent. She'd been too distracted to notice, but she had been sitting alongside Everett Wooten all along.

"Mr. Wooten?" she asked in astonishment. At his nod she turned to Colin. "But he doesn't seem so bad."

Colin blanched, and she wished she could call the words back. How awful to insult this man who'd only been kind to her. Maybe he didn't notice her gaffe?

But he did. His face became closed and shuttered. He stiffly leaned down to begin gathering the scattered candy into a tidier mound. "I'd better go ask for another bag at the front desk."

He left without another word and Colin sat beside her on the bench. "What was all that about?" he asked.

Mary relayed what Mr. Wooten mentioned about having a cook who had the same nervous condition and how a paper bag could help. There had been no time for introductions, and now she'd gotten the relationship off on a terrible footing.

Mr. Wooten returned with another bag and squatted down to fill it with the candy. His face was expressionless as he filled the bag. "Why haven't you been answering my letters?"

The steel bands surrounding her chest tightened, and she was on the verge of another attack. Her heart raced and breathing became difficult again, but somehow just holding the paper bag in her hands gave an odd sort of comfort.

"I thought they were weekly reports."

"You still don't read the weekly reports I send?"

How to answer that? They were filled with nothing but charts and percentages and projections. She didn't know what to make of them and had complete confidence in his abilities to manage the company. All she cared about was that quarterly infusion of cash.

"I need to do better," she admitted.

The candy was collected and Mr. Wooten stood. "Call me Everett," he said bluntly. "We need to discuss the case. I haven't had dinner yet. Will you join me?"

"Excellent idea," Colin said. "The leek soup here is beyond compare."

Colin was always quite the gourmand when it came to dining and she'd trust his judgment. A maître d' led them into a wood-paneled dining room filled with the warm scents of fresh bread, garlic, and braised beef. The lights were dim but a crackling fireplace on one side of the room provided cozy illumination among the clinking china and soft voices.

But they weren't here to dine, they were here to avoid being evicted from their ancestral home. She'd let Colin lead the discussion, for he surely had the best instincts for business.

"What are your recommendations for tonight?" Colin asked the maître d' after they were all seated.

"The chef recommends the leek soup, which is always a favorite, and for dinner the baked lobster has been prepared with garlic butter and an au gratin finish of toasted breadcrumbs, fresh herbs, and grated parmesan cheese."

Colin didn't even look at the menu but simply handed it back to the maître d' with a smile. "Excellent. I'll have as you suggest. Mary?"

"The same."

The maître d' turned to Everett, who scrutinized the menu as though it was the Rosetta Stone, taking an inordinately long time before ordering. "I'll have the pumpkin soup for starters," he finally said. "For the main course the chicken with the orange glaze, with a side of carrots."

Across the candlelit table, Mary caught Colin's gaze. Every item Everett just ordered was orange. The apricot candy he sampled in the lobby had been orange, too. Curiosity clawed at her. She was dying to know if it was true that he only ate one color of food per day. She opened her mouth to ask, but Colin guessed what she was thinking and gave a tiny shake of his head to dissuade her.

Her curiosity got worse when the men ordered from the bar, for while Colin settled for a small tumbler of spiced rum, Everett ordered a Grand Marnier. She had little experience with spirits, but when the drinks arrived, Everett's drink was a deep orange.

She couldn't help herself. "I'm not familiar with Grand Marnier," she said. "What can you tell me about it?"

"It's a French cognac," Everett said. "Flavored with the peel of bitter orange and a little sugar. I don't particularly care for it."

"Then why did you order it?"

Everett wiggled the glass, observing the jewel-toned liquid in the candlelight like a scientist. "I like to try different things," he said. "Now, let's get down to business. It seems Whitefriars is in financial distress, and I—"

"What makes you think so?" Colin interrupted.

"Why else would you be advertising to lease out rooms?"

Colin turned to her. She'd rather die than admit the truth, but it wouldn't be lying to say the influx of cash would be welcome. "The rye fields no longer yield the revenue they once did."

Everett's brows lowered in concern. "But we discussed this. Didn't you implement the drainage pump I recommended?"

"I did. Thank you for the recommendation, for it's been working like a charm. As far back as I can remember the south fields have been waterlogged, but now—"

"So what's the problem? If your fields aren't performing, you should have written to me. I can help."

"It isn't that. I'm afraid the price of rye has been falling for decades, and no advice can solve that."

"Nonsense. I purchase raw food staples from all over the world, and there are ways to order commodities for bulk pricing. Or take creative advantage of international tariffs. You should have consulted me. Haven't I always offered help in the past?"

He did, but she couldn't imagine he'd could have any insight into the price of rye. In hindsight, that was foolish. This man probably bought and sold more rye in a year than Whitefriars sold in decades.

"I see now that I should have," she admitted. "I thought the simple leasing of a few rooms in the castle could be a reliable form of revenue that can—"

"It's unacceptable, and a violation of the contract your brother signed with my father."

"How so?" Colin asked.

"It cheapens the image of the castle. My father and I built a luxury brand of food products on the Whitefriars name and reputation. We invested a fortune in that image."

A waiter interrupted the conversation to deliver the first course. What a welcome reprieve, for Everett's rapid-fire form of discussion was alarming. The ritual of grinding pepper and sprinkling additional grated cheese atop their soup further slowed the conversation, but too soon the waiter left, and they were back to business.

"Inviting guests to stay in our home does not impact the reputation of Whitefriars," Colin pointed out.

Everett's voice was sharp. "Vaudeville performers?"

"Vaudeville?" she asked. "What are you talking about?"

"Robbie and Carlotta Bannister. They run the largest and tackiest vaudeville show in America, and now they're bragging up and down the East Coast that they are staying at Whitefriars for the entire month of February."

Mary took a spoonful of soup to play for time. She knew nothing of the Bannisters other than the pleasant correspondence she'd exchanged with Carlotta Bannister to make the arrangements, and they'd already paid in full. She'd worried she set too high an asking price, especially for a dismal month like February, but the Bannisters paid without a hint of haggling. She hadn't known how they earned their money, nor did she care.

"It materially effects the value of the Whitefriars image," Everett continued. "The Bannisters are famous for their travelling freak show. Two-headed cats, wrestling ladies, dwarf shows. This is not the sort of image I can permit to be associated with Whitefriars."

Colin cleared his throat and shot her an annoyed glare. "My apologies. I did not realize the Bannisters had made reservations at Whitefriars."

Given the chill on Colin's face, she had committed quite a blunder in accepting their reservation. How was she to know of the Bannisters' reputation? She'd never stepped foot outside of England. All she knew was that Mrs. Bannister was perfectly polite and willing to pay in full. Those funds had already been spent to re-gravel the front drive, which had been a shockingly expensive endeavor given that the front drive was more than a mile long.

Colin and Everett continued discussing the matter and she tried to pay attention, but it was hard to concentrate while reliving how difficult it had been to re-gravel the drive. She was proud of that work! Most of it had been done by laborers, but she had personally helped level the ground and pulled roots to save some of the cost. And now Colin complained.

A waiter arrived with their meal, which caused the conversation to cease while plates were exchanged. The sight of Everett's plate of orange food did little to reassure her that he could be rational, but he'd been kind to her out in the lobby. He helped a stranger in distress, and even though he'd been a little stiff, she must not overlook that.

"If we extricated ourselves from the Bannister reservation, would that satisfy your concerns?" Colin asked once the waiter retreated.

"The Bannisters are only the beginning of the problem," Everett replied. "I object to using the building upon which I built a company to be rented out to the highest bidder. It tarnishes the estate."

"I would never do anything to tarnish Whitefriars," she said. Her work restoring it was the only thing of which she truly was proud. "I wish you understood Whitefriars as I do. It began as a cloister for Cistercian monks over a thousand years ago. Back then it was only a wooden monastery that's long gone, and the land has changed hands many times over the years. The first stage of the castle was built in the fourteenth century. Whitefriars is over five hundred years of history and thousands of lives. I'd give anything to know more about those people who once lived there. Colin says I'm crazy, but I can sense them as I walk the grounds or explore the castle. It's impossible to know their individual stories, but I know they were there, and they fought in great, magnificent causes. I will always honor them."

She looked at Everett, surprised by the hint of curiosity on his face. It gave her the courage to continue. "The monks who founded Whitefriars dedicated their lives to prayer and caring for the poor. Henry VIII seized Whitefriars in 1538 during the dissolution of the monasteries, and a hundred years later it was awarded to the Beckwiths by a grateful King James for military service. During the civil war the baron risked his life to give shelter to fleeing royalists. But it wasn't all warfare and strife. Centuries went by when people fought to save a harvest or raise their children. In the seventeenth century the great hall was used as a hospital during the cholera outbreak. This estate is a microcosm of England itself. I would never do anything to cheapen the memory of the people who lived here. They inspire me. I want to be as big and bold as the people who've gone before me. Don't laugh, Colin… I'm serious."

"I know you are," her brother said, then turned to Everett, a hint of amusement still lingering on his face. "She still pulls weeds and lays wreaths on the monks' graves. We're Protestants, so my father thought it heresy to be honoring the Catholic monks like that, but she still does it."

Perhaps they were getting sidetracked, but Everett seemed curious, so she continued. "Sometimes late at night I can almost hear the echo of the people who've come before me. Every now and then I stumble across faint traces of them. Someone's initials carved on an old wall or scribbling in the margins of a book. Once I found a baby's rattle with little marks on the teething stem. I wonder about the baby who left those teeth marks and what became of him. It's a blessing and a privilege to be the caretaker of this estate."

"I'd like to see it," Everett said.

"Please, come!" she said. If he saw Whitefriars in person, it would be clear she wasn't cheapening the grand estate. "You can have the tower rooms and be our very first guest."

Everett extracted a compact leather book from his breast pocket, consulting it with a frown on his face. "I am in town for three more days. Tomorrow will be spent touring confectioneries, but I can visit the day after that, if it would be convenient?"

"Excellent," Colin said, and Mary felt an easing of the tension in her spine. Perhaps Everett was a normal man who could be reasoned with after all!

The maître d' arrived with the menu card for dessert, and as usual, he volunteered the bakery chef's personal recommendations. "May I suggest the chocolate and raspberry torte? It is a masterpiece of bittersweet French cocoa infused with sweet vanilla cream and a fresh raspberry glaze."

"It sounds marvelous," she said, and Colin agreed.

Everett did not. "I'll have the orange sherbet, please."

***

Mary began strategizing the moment the carriage door pulled closed. "Everything has to be perfect," she said, her teeth chattering from a combination of the icy night air and nervousness over the impending visit.

Colin mercifully agreed. "We'll clear the broken equipment out of the stables and burn it if we must. Let's go ahead and cut pine boughs and drape the railings in the great hall. It might distract from the fact that the staircase is still rickety."

"Can you wire to New York for his food schedule?" At Colin's befuddled look, she clarified. "You told me he only eats one color of food a day, and that his colors come in order. Today was orange. Heaven help us if he visits on a blue or purple day, but I shall make sure we can accommodate him. I need to know so that Mrs. Galloway can have the necessary ingredients on hand."

"Serving him blue food isn't going to save Whitefriars,"

Colin said dryly. "We need to prove we haven't cheapened its image in preparing to lease the tower."

"Nothing I've done is cheap, believe me. Could you please wire to New York and get to that man who told you about Mr. Wooten's penchant for colored food?"

Colin had a telegraph wire installed in Whitefriars decades ago. As a boy, he'd taught himself Morse code to listen to cricket scores and news of the world on their isolated, wind-swept estate. Mary never needed an escape. Tramping through the woods and attics of Whitefriars was enough to fire her imagination with speculation about the monks, the warriors, the lords and ladies who'd lived there over the centuries.

"I'll wire, but please don't pin your hopes on this. Everett Wooten is all about the returns on his financial investments, and we can't afford to forget it."

CHAPTER THREE

EVERETT COULD HAVE kicked himself for giving in to the momentary surge of attraction to Mary Beckwith that prompted his agreement to stay overnight at Whitefriars. He'd been unexpectedly moved by her passion for the estate, but that was no reason to lose his mind and endanger the pending deals he had percolating in Berlin and New York City.

And yet, he'd done it. Thirty-five years of business-like and responsible behavior, and he chucked it away because a pretty lady spoke movingly about the privilege of tending some monks' graves. Now he was going to have to endure two days of small talk with strangers, and there were few things on this planet he disliked more than small talk. The soirees his mother made him attend had always been pure torture. Laughing young ladies and useless men of leisure indulging in witty repartee, while he stood about feeling big, awkward, and out of place. He once even bought a book of etiquette for gentlemen to glean insight into the mysterious art of conversation. None of it worked. While his mother was alive he attended her parties and socialized like other men of his class, but it had been hard. Very hard. She died three years ago, and he hadn't been to a weekend party or time-wasting soiree since.

Now here he was, trapped in a carriage on his way to Whitefriars. To make it worse, he'd been told several Beckwith relatives from America were also visiting, making the entire endeavor seem uncomfortably like a weekend house party.

But he needed to investigate Whitefriars. Too much of his business depended on the image of Whitefriars that was engraved on the label of every jar of food he sold.

A gatehouse arched over the entrance, two buildings framing the road joined by an enclosed passageway stretching over the path. Even after passing through the gatehouse he still couldn't see the castle. Towering oaks and juniper trees lined the drive that curved through the land. Every now and then a break in the trees showed fields of winter wheat, looking healthy and well-established for December. A faint smile threatened, for he'd consulted a number of experts when Mary first wrote to him of the problem with waterlogged fields. He loved solving problems, and by all accounts his recommendations for draining the land had been successful.

The carriage rounded a bend and Whitefriars loomed before him. The castle sprawled across two acres, a hodge-podge of different styles cobbled together over the centuries. A square central building was flanked by two wings, three spires, and a large tower. The castle was built of honeyed stone with mullioned windows that sparkled in the sunlight, looking grand and stately in the barren winter landscape.

As the carriage rounded another bend, he was able to see the silhouette that had been made famous on millions of pricey jars of sauces and jams. He rapped on the carriage to ask the driver to stop, for he'd prefer to walk these last few acres. It would give him the chance to inspect the grounds.

The drive looked freshly graveled, but a few of the outbuildings visible through the leafless trees were ramshackle and dilapidated. Those couldn't be helped. He'd paid a fortune to restore the actual castle, but nothing toward the outbuildings. It was another reason he didn't want visitors here. If people got a close look at the estate, it would be like peeling the curtain back to reveal decline and decay. Not things he wanted associated with his pricey line of gourmet food.

He tugged on his collar to flip it up against the frigid wind. The air smelled good. Piney. Maybe a little peat. Altogether much nicer than Manhattan, which smelled like wet pavement at this time of year.

The front door opened and Colin stepped outside, sending him a hearty wave. Everett muttered a curse, his last few minutes of privacy gone, for others had gathered alongside Colin. They waved, smiled, and called out greetings. He sank a little farther into his coat, wishing they hadn't all assembled in such an intimidating group. It was going to be a long weekend.

"Welcome to Whitefriars!" Colin called out as he came striding down the path toward him and extended his hand.

Everett returned the handshake. "Thank you. It's good to finally see the place."

"Come in out of the cold. You look freezing." The others had already retreated behind the massive front door, and all too soon he joined them. Lots of people, including two young women holding toddlers.

Mary looked as elegant as a cameo, her pale complexion in stark contrast to her glossy dark hair. She looked so refined, not at all like the effusive and sentimental woman who waxed with poetic nostalgia the other evening. What on earth prompted him to give in to the momentary jolt of insanity? Mary Beckwith was precisely the sort of polished, high-society lady he always avoided.

Colin performed the introductions. "You've already met Mary, and have you met my wife, Lucy?"

He nodded, for he remembered Lucy Beckwith well. A pretty lady with brown hair and sparkling brown eyes, she came from a working-class background and carried no airs. "We met at my mother's Independence Day bash in Central Park," he said. That had been four years ago, back when Everett still felt obligated to attend such events.

"I remember," Lucy said. "And this is my brother, Nick, and his wife, Rosalind. And their children. Sadie is seven and baby Jake is eighteen months this week."

Nick was the commissioner of water for the state of New York and up to his neck in politics, labor unions, and rabble-rousers. His wife was a petite woman with silvery-blond hair and seemed dainty, shy, and, mercifully, did not expect him to talk.

"How was your trip from town?" Colin asked congenially.

"Bumpy. Cold." It was cold in here, too. The great hall had a huge, vaulted ceiling where most of the heat was surely hiding. Their voices echoed off the stone and he couldn't imagine why anyone would want to live in such a place.

"Let's head into the parlor for some refreshments," Mary suggested. "Perhaps afterward I can provide a tour of the castle?"

"That would be nice."

What a brilliant rejoinder, but he couldn't think of anything more interesting to say. Everyone laughed and talked as they headed down an arched stone corridor, but the parlor was a relief. The room had a low ceiling, newly plastered walls, and a bank of windows overlooking a pond. A thick rug, upholstered furnishings, and a cheery fireplace warmed the room. It was clearly one of the newer parts of the castle and had benefitted from a complete restoration.

"Please have a seat," Mary said, gesturing to the tall-backed chair before the fireplace. "And look! Refreshments have arrived."

A maid wheeled in a cart weighed down with a tea service and several platters of delicacies. It seemed like everyone was holding their breath, waiting for his reaction. He glanced at the tea cart. Blueberry tarts, wedges of blue cheese, petit fours with blue icing, a dish of little blue candies. He swallowed hard.

Were they making fun of him? This wasn't a coincidence, and everyone was waiting for his reaction and he didn't know what to do.

"Perhaps just some tea," he said.

"Excellent," Mary replied in a bright voice. "Let's see. We have borage tea, elderberry tea, or plain black tea."

"I'll have the plain black tea."

It seemed no one wanted either of the two blue tea options. Just as well, for they weren't very good, but Mary seemed befuddled that he hadn't pounced on the blue tea. He listened politely as Colin and Mary carried the conversation. At first he tried to think of something to say, but aside from business, he simply had nothing in common with these people. It was only ten minutes into his visit and he already regretted coming. Perhaps if he could conclude his inspection of the castle and the grounds quickly, he could cut the visit short. He certainly didn't want any of the blue food they rolled out with such fanfare.

There was a lull in the conversation and he set his teacup down. "Perhaps now would be a good time to tour the castle?"

"Of course," Mary said brightly. "The entire central area and the east wing have been completely renovated. I can show you the kitchens, the music room, the two parlors, and—"

"I'd like to see the tower rooms, please." He trusted that the renovated part of the castle was fine, but it was the tower being offered for lease, and the only part he truly needed to see. Mary seemed a little hurt, but he wanted to move quickly. With luck he could wrap up his business in a few hours and be back in York by this evening.

It seemed everyone wanted to show him the tower room, for they all trailed after him as Mary escorted him down another of the stone-lined corridors. The floors had been worn smooth from centuries of feet, and the air carried only the tiniest hint of dank. One couldn't expect better of an old castle.

A chain on Mary's waist had a set of keys. The tower room had its own lock, quite appropriate for guests who required privacy, but hopefully it would never come to that. He walked a few paces behind, deliberately slowing his steps for a better view of Mary's slim form, admiring the way she almost glided down the hallway, her skirts swaying in a gentle motion. Inane thoughts of a medieval chatelaine walking the halls struck him. No wonder Mary found it easy to lapse into reveries about the people who'd lived here long ago.

"Here we are," Mary said, stepping inside and holding the door for him. It was nice inside, the scent of fresh plaster still in the air. Despite the tapestry on the wall and a large rug covering the floor, it was still chilly.

The others followed him inside, and the uncomfortable sensation of being watched was back. Everyone was waiting for his opinion, as though he was a judge about to hand down a ruling.

"Nice," he said noncommittally. The first rule of business was to never let the opposition know what you were thinking. It had always been easy to play his cards close to the chest, and he held to that standard now.

"This can be a gathering room for guests," Mary said, stepping to a window to pull the draperies wide. "You see the view? I should think guests from London or New York would pay a lot to enjoy a view like that."

People didn't cross an ocean for a view. "It's very cold in here. Is there no heat?"

"We can lay a fire," Colin said cheerfully. "All part of the Cromwellian charm."

He'd prefer some Sears Roebuck charm. The department store sold gas heaters for thirty dollars and this place could use one.

"Let's see upstairs."

Both of the upper-levels were fully renovated with new floors, plastered walls, and furniture that was new and charming. Mary was saying something about needing to scuff up the furniture to reflect the age of the castle. It sounded like sheer nonsense if she'd asked him, but she hadn't.

It was obvious she'd spent a lot of time and money renovating this tower, but she hadn't asked him a single thing about this scheme to prostitute the castle. After all the advice he'd provided over the years, she hadn't thought to give him the simple courtesy of advance notice regarding her plans.

He mustn't let offended feelings interfere with his assessment of the property. Rule number two of business: Don't get emotionally involved. As he turned to face the others, five people watched him, tense and anxious. Every one of them was emotionally invested in this property, which made their judgment questionable. He wasn't in the business of saving the Beckwith family heritage, he was here to safeguard the reputation of his company.

"Let's see the top floor, please."

A momentary hint of disappointment flashed across Mary's face, but she smiled and turned to lead the way upstairs.

The top floor had a breathtaking view from both bedrooms and the sitting area. The master bedroom was especially impressive, with a large bed, a dressing table, and two walnut wardrobes, but his eye was drawn to a small door.

"What's behind the door?" he asked, curious because it had a lock on it. Closets were such an American feature and he doubted she would add one, especially since the room had plenty of wardrobe space.

"That's a staircase leading to the attic. The ceiling was too low to make it usable, so it hasn't been renovated."

"I'd like to see it, please."

Mary twisted her hands. "It won't show the castle in the best light. There's nothing to see up there, and only tiny slits for light. It's a bit of a junk collection, I'm afraid."

All the more reason for him to see it. If the attic was a moldering ruin, the smell of rot would eventually taint the rest of the rooms. Mary looked resigned as she stepped forward with her set of keys, summoning those disconcerting analogies of the medieval chatelaine again.

One look at the staircase was all he needed to understand why she hadn't wanted him to see it. Crumbling masonry, a dangerously low ceiling, and no railing on the bare stone walls made it look decrepit and dangerous. Nevertheless, he wanted to see the attic.

Mary advised the attic was too small to hold them all and suggested the others go finish their tea in the parlor. The blue tea. None of them had touched any of the blue delicacies earlier, and they'd probably chuck them out now that he'd decided not to play their game.

He ducked low to follow Mary up to the attic, where the air was so stale he could almost taste it. Narrow slits for windows had probably once been used for archers defending the castle. Now they let in light but added no charm. He cautiously straightened. The ceiling was a scant two inches above his head, but he could stand without hunching over. A glance around the space revealed battered trunks, rusted iron equipment, and a one-eyed doll propped against the wall. He pulled the doll aside, relieved to see no mouse droppings or mold blooms behind it.

"Satisfied?" Mary asked.

"No. Not at all."

She stared at him in disbelief. "What exactly were you expecting to see up here?"

It was a fair question, and he didn't want to examine his motives too closely, for he had no legitimate cause to feel hurt. They had been exchanging letters for nine years. On the surface, their letters were only about business, but he'd always viewed them as a delightfully productive correspondence that let him help in the challenging work of restoring an estate.

"I'm still trying to figure out why you embarked on this reckless scheme to begin with," he said. "You should have come to me. When have I ever failed to help when you turned to me?"

"I have no idea what you're going on about."

"I helped you with the drainage problem. When you feared being cheated on the roof, I sent out specialists to resolve the problem. When you ran out of money for new windows, I paid for the glaziers."

"I've said I will pay you back for that."

"Forget about the money," he snapped. He started to pace, like he always did when frustrated, but there wasn't enough room up here. "This entire castle is a financial sinkhole, but my father negotiated the deal, and it's my job to ensure it pays off in the long run. It was a stupid, foolhardy investment that bought us nothing but an overpriced emblem to slap on our jars and precious little else. No one in America even knows Whitefriars, but now, thanks to you, they think of it as the place the Bannister Vaudeville company goes to vacation. If you needed funds, you should have come to me. When have I ever let you down?"

He shouldn't have insulted Whitefriars. Her eyes looked like blue pools of wounded feelings, and guilt ate at him, but he needed an answer. "When, Mary?"

She blinked rapidly. "You haven't. I made a mistake."

He turned away to avoid the naked pain in her face but bumped his shin on a ratty old bed frame. "Let's go downstairs to discuss this in the Cromwellian charm of the main floor.

Your family makes me nervous, but I think we can talk this out between the two of us."

She nodded and led the way out of the attic. They'd have to move quickly if he was going to wrap this up in time to get back to the city tonight. He wouldn't have minded the chance to get to know her better, but he didn't like her family. Too many people, all staring at him, testing him.

Unless he'd misinterpreted the situation. It wouldn't be the first time, and prudence dictated that he clarify what was going on.

"Why the blue food?" he asked once they were in the tower's first-floor parlor.

Mary turned to him, a helpless look of resignation on her face. "We heard a rumor. I guess it's true?"

"That I eat only one color per day?"

"That's the one." Her face was flooded with embarrassment and she rushed to apologize, babbling so quickly he feared she might descend into another of those attacks of panic.

"Stop," he said. "Sit. This isn't worth getting upset over."

She complied, lowering herself onto the padded sofa, and he tugged a footstool over so he could be close enough to hear if her breathing got caught in the vicious loop.

"It started out as a bet I had with my father," he said, anything to distract her from the looming panic. "We're in the food business, and curious about what people find appealing. We charge an outrageous price for Whitefriars products."

"Because they're the best," Mary said, and this time his smile was genuine. There were *so many* ways he could respond to that. True, their quality was top-notch. Same with the packaging. But he charged five times the price of production and that's what made the Whitefriars line of products a true business marvel. Very few companies could afford to set that kind of premium price, and he had to protect their reputation. Mary still seemed on edge and there was no need for that.

"It was just a silly bet between me and Dad to see if we could think of enough green food to make a well-rounded meal. Then it grew. A day of red food, blue food, and so on."

Frank Wooten was more than just his father. He was the only real friend he had, but they were both competitive men and both in the food business. It was a challenge to come up with new and different foods to keep the bet alive, and it was run entirely on the honor system. They indulged in the bet only about one week each month, but it had been going on for years. Everett would obviously lose this round due to the trip to Whitefriars, and he tried to reassure Mary there was no need to cater to his odd food-color wager.

"You shouldn't have to lose just because of this trip," Mary said. "We'll help! Whatever you need."

"Truly, I'd prefer if you didn't." He was here on business, not to make new friends or win a bet. It was hard enough being plunged into a group of strangers without being the focus of attention. "This estate and its reputation are very important to my business. The exterior of the house looks sound, but the gardens are shoddy and several outbuildings are in poor condition. Especially that one right there." He pointed out the window, for the tumbled-down structure was less than an acre from the castle and a pitiful eyesore. Three stone walls were standing, but one was entirely gone and the roof looked ready to collapse any moment.

"That ruin looks like somewhere for vagrants to set up camp. It should be torn down." Given Mary's reaction, he'd just blundered again. "I'm sorry that I spoke so bluntly. I keep forgetting this is your home."

He'd never seen a woman so sensitive, for it looked like he'd just suggested a family member be thrown onto a pyre. She never seemed this sentimental in her letters, which were to the point, articulate, and eager for his help.

"I love the bakehouse," she said. "I used to play in it as a child."

It was a blot on the landscape. Whitefriars wasn't a child's playground, it was a business investment, and the bakehouse would have to go. There'd be time to discuss it later, but for now he simply wanted to listen to Mary talk. Her voice was soothing. He could listen to her ramble for hours.

"Tell me more about the outbuildings," he said, and she immediately brightened. By heavens, she could talk. He chose a more comfortable seat as she relayed the history of the bakehouse, the gatehouse, and a dovecote, which was a tiny little building kept only for doves. He tried not to laugh, for it might discourage her breathlessly frank conversation, but rich people in England were very different than rich Americans. His sister had an entire room for her shoes, but even his sister would be astonished at a tiny stone castle spire created to house doves.

Mary spoke of a watermill and how they used to mill their own grain for themselves and neighborhood farms. That came to an end when their land became so waterlogged their crops dwindled to nothing. The miller moved away, the mill fell into disuse, and bats made themselves at home in the eaves.

"Now that our fields are productive, I would love to see that mill back in operation," she said.

"How much will it cost to restore?" He couldn't help

himself. His mind latched on to the possible return on the investment and downstream revenue opportunities. Mary had already gathered preliminary costs for getting the watermill back in operation, and he saw an entirely new facet to her as she began strategizing for future improvements.

It seemed Mary wasn't merely passionate about Whitefriars' history, but its business potential as well, and that made her even more attractive. He'd never met a woman so comfortable discussing business. Not that he'd met all that many women. He put great effort into avoiding social engagements, and ever since his engagement to Stella Rowland collapsed, he didn't even try to mingle with the fairer sex.

Two hours passed while he chatted with Mary about the history of the estate. It wasn't wasted time, for now he could better converse with business associates about the estate that served as the emblem of the Whitefriars brand.

A glance out the window showed the afternoon shadows growing long. The sun set early this far north, and it had crept up on him unawares.

"I've forgotten how short the days are here," he admitted. "It looks as if I will have to stay overnight after all."

"Wasn't that always the plan?" she asked.

He didn't want to admit the shameful desire to flee the estate as soon as possible. It was so much easier to make use of a hotel rather than be a guest among strangers. Except Mary didn't feel like a stranger. From the moment he saw her in the lobby of the Knightsbridge Inn he simply felt at ease with her. The attraction didn't warrant too much attention, for it could come to nothing. His father depended on him, as did three hundred employees working for the company. He had ambitious plans for expansion, and they needed his daily attention.

And since Mary was inextricably linked to Whitefriars, there was no point in entertaining daydreams of what could be. Mary was a business associate who was the caretaker of Whitefriars, nothing more.

"Yes," he said, "that was always the plan. I'll carry my bags up to the top floor."

***

Mary raced to join the others, who were enjoying tea in the parlor. Everett was still unpacking his bags in the tower room, so they didn't have long. The blue food was untouched, all expect the blueberry pie, which was entirely consumed.

"Cancel the white food for tomorrow. He knows what we're doing and doesn't like it."

Nick looked amused. "What are we going to do with two gallons of white sauce?"

"Pretend to be Cleopatra and take a bath in it," she said in frustration. "In the meantime, pray for good weather tomorrow. He wants to inspect the outbuildings. I think he's willing to have them renovated."

Colin stood by the fireplace, hands shoved in his pockets and brooding. "I don't like taking on more debt."

"And I want to get the bakehouse restored. The crops don't earn enough to pay for it, so I need you to help me make a good impression on Everett."

"Mary, shall we go for a little walk along the parapet? I could use some fresh air."

All her senses went on alert, for Colin had adopted the

casual deportment of a gentleman at leisure. He was so good at the sangfroid routine, but she could tell he was angry and didn't want to air it before the others. Neither did she, so she led the way.

The parapet was a bumpy walk atop on old section of wall that joined the renovated section of the castle with the unrenovated section built in the fifteenth century. It had a splendid view of the grounds, but a chill blew through the air and Colin's voice was grim.

"Three days ago this man was threatening to repossess the estate. Now you've spent an afternoon in his company and think he's the mortgage fairy? Father Christmas bearing gifts? Don't let your guard down. He can still pull the trigger on that clause in the contract at any time. Why don't you just promise him you won't lease the tower? We don't need the money."

She kept walking, an angry rush of words swirling inside. Someone like Colin couldn't understand. From the time they were children, Colin was brave and outgoing, surrounded by friends, the most popular man in any school, weekend party, or gentlemen's club. While she loved having him here for Christmas, in a week he and all the others would go back to New York, leaving her to roll around this big empty building like a marble in a box. Entirely alone except for a cook, a few stable hands, and a maid from the village who came four days a week. They were employees, not family. It was hard to exist year after year without the warmth and affection of real friends and family. These two weeks at Christmas had to sustain her for the entire year.

"Please don't be cross," she said. "Christmas is my favorite season and I don't want to spoil it with arguments."

"And I don't want to spoil it with an eviction."

She bit her tongue to stop from lashing out. In theory, Colin knew everything she'd done to hold this castle together, but he'd never once risen before dawn to milk the goats or stayed awake through the night to battle rain pouring in through a collapsed ceiling. He never sneezed himself into a migraine while washing moldy tapestries or risked his sanity chasing bats out of the attic. She crossed her arms and glared at the landscape.

Yes, the watermill looked bad, but she found tenants for it and she loved their company. Likewise, the tenants she found for the gatehouse. Those people were close to being real friends and if she could get the bakehouse fixed, she could lease that, too.

Colin pointed toward the mill. "The rubble piled outside the watermill looks ramshackle," he said. "So does the roof of the gatehouse. I agree with Everett that you shouldn't be leasing the tower while the grounds look this bad. Wait until the place is presentable before you start stuffing the castle with guests."

The cork popped off the roiling cauldron of resentment. "That's very easy for you to say with your multitude of friends and family and babies and fine life in New York. I'm grateful for the revenue from the licensing deal, but Colin! Honestly! You ran off to New York and got married without a word to me! You left me to run this crumbling old estate all by myself. Do you know how terrified I was? How alone and overwhelmed? All the responsibility was on me, and I've decided to lease the tower so I can have a smidgeon of human companionship instead of talking to myself like a madwoman shut up in a castle."

Colin's face went white, his mouth a hard line of

disapproval. "I didn't think I needed to consult my little sister about my choice of a wife."

He should have if it meant he'd live on the other side of the ocean, but she clamped her mouth shut. She'd already said too much, casting a pall over her favorite time of year.

"Let's go rejoin the others," she said. "I don't think we are going to convince each other."

Colin said nothing as he followed her back inside, but she could sense him bristling the entire way.

CHAPTER FOUR

EVERETT FOUND THE tower a truly miserable place to spend the night. It was freezing, drafty, and noisy. Only minutes after he opened a book and settled in to read, animals in the chimney began scrabbling about, scratching and thumping. It was surprisingly vigorous, keeping him awake for hours. A fire was out of the question lest he smoke and cook whatever was nesting in the chimney.

He dragged every coverlet from the armoire to mound atop the bed, but it seemed that each time he began settling in, the wind began howling, whistling through cracks in the newly installed windows. Part of him wanted to ignore it, especially since the wind increased the chill in the room, but he couldn't. It shouldn't be too difficult to seal these leaks, but they needed to be identified. He climbed from beneath the warmth of the blankets to shiver while running his palms along the windowsills, side jambs, and casing in search of the leaks. He'd note the spots and report them later.

He knew in his soul the first thing Mary was going to ask tomorrow morning. With her sunny disposition she would cast him one of those blinding smiles and ask, "How was your night in the tower?"

He burrowed back under the covers, his hands and feet icy. He would be polite if it killed him. He'd say lots of nice things before pointing out the leaky windows and the need for a chimney sweep to scare out the critters. Why anyone would cross the ocean to live in a damp, drafty castle was a mystery, but Mary seemed convinced it was a good investment. Meanwhile, each additional day he stagnated in rural isolation was damaging to his business. There were factories to tour and new technologies to license, none of which he could accomplish in a run-down castle in Yorkshire.

He woke cold and bleary-eyed as the sun rose. The room was still wickedly cold, but if the fireplace had been going it wouldn't have been so intolerable. A glance out one of the windows showed two field hands out near a goat pen. He'd let one of them know about the chimney and hopefully it could be remedied immediately. He didn't expect to spend another night here, but if he did, he wanted a fire.

He dressed and headed toward the great hall, where it was so frigid and empty he could see his breath in the air and even hear his heartbeat. Every footstep echoed off the stone walls and vaulted ceiling, mingling with the laughing voices from the far-off parlor.

Mercifully, he was able to avoid everyone and escape through the front doors and onto the grounds. He blew on his hands to warm them, climbing up and over a berm on his way to the stable block and barn. Two horses grazed in the field, and a dozen goats clustered around a feed trough. A pair of farm hands had one goat pulled aside. One man held it steady while the other milked it. They probably weren't the right people to sweep the chimney, but they would know someone who could.

"Excuse me!" he hollered.

The one milking the goat turned around and he nearly choked. Of all the things he expected of Mary Beckwith, seeing her milk a goat had not been on the list. She patted the goat's haunch, then stood and loped over toward him.

"Good morning!" she said cheerfully. No wonder he'd mistaken her for a boy. She wore trousers, a battered old jacket, and muddy work boots. Her hair was pinned beneath a woolen cap, but her smile was as sunny as ever.

"How was the tower room?" she asked. "You were our inaugural guest!"

She looked so eager for his opinion it was hard to disappoint her, but she needed to know. "The chimney will need a good cleaning before a fire can be lit. You've got critters living in it."

Her face fell. "You must have been freezing!"

He was, but she looked plenty cold too, her gloveless fingers bright red in the frosty morning air. He had to admire a woman not too proud to dirty her hands with milking duties. He nodded to the goats. "Is this something you do regularly?"

"Only when I'm needed," she said. "Two of our hands have gone to the city to be with their family for Christmas, so I'm helping out until they get back in January. Don't worry. I'll find someone to sweep the chimney today."

"You won't be the one to do it, right?" He would sweep it himself before letting a lady climb onto the roof on his behalf.

"Oscar can do it," she said with a nod to the man who

had taken over milking duties. "Come! Let me show you the grounds, for that's why you came all this way."

A fierce northerly wind was blowing, making it uncomfortable to be outdoors, but this was his last chance to get a good look at the sorry state of the outbuildings. Asserting his majority ownership of the property would be awkward, but he'd do whatever was necessary to protect the Whitefriars image. He raised the collar of his coat as they headed down the path, for the wind seemed to cut straight through to his skin.

Mary noticed. "I'm sure Colin will loan you a scarf if you need one."

"I'm fine," he said, trying to ignore the charm of her smile. It would be better if they could stick to business. He'd never been comfortable around women, but Mary had a way of getting to him and he mustn't let his guard down.

"Let's see that bakehouse you were telling me about."

The hard ground was covered with a layer of frost, but it didn't take long to arrive at the crumbling remnants of a bakehouse. It was around the size of a railroad car, with stone walls on three sides and completely open to the elements on the fourth. A fireplace filled one wall, and when he approached it a squirrel darted from beneath the shriveled leaves mounded in the fireplace. It was a crumbling medieval ruin, a complete wreck, but Mary was defensive on its behalf.

"It never had a fourth wall," she explained. "Bakehouses are usually wide open, otherwise they get too hot. There was a time when this bakehouse made countless loaves of bread to feed the entire county."

Being open to the elements for hundreds of years had wrought plenty of damage. The stone pavers on the ground were buckled, dirt was encrusted into every crevice, and the roof had gaps letting sunlight through.

"What are your intentions for this bakehouse? Yesterday you mentioned adding a bunch of windows onto a fourth wall. That seems an odd choice."

"I think it could become an atelier," she said. "That's a fancy French term for an artist's studio. I heard that in France some of the estates make room for an artist on their grounds, and plenty of light is the most important thing for an artist. If I'm building the wall anyway, I might as well build it with plenty of windows so that if I ever decide to lease it to an artist, it will be suitable."

"But why?" he pressed, utterly baffled. Most artists were poor as church mice, not like the obscenely wealthy people she hoped would lease the tower.

She laid her hand on the stone ledge over the fireplace as she gazed into space. "I like the idea of having an artist live here. A painter or a sculptor. And if that person is married perhaps there would be children, too. There is plenty of room for living quarters, and there's already a fireplace."

She whirled to look at him. "But it doesn't have to be an artist! I merely like the idea of resurrecting Whitefriars to something like it used to be long ago. A community. People with different blessings and skills all finding a home here. I've already leased the millhouse and the gatehouse, and I'm sure I can find a tenant for the bakehouse once it's been restored."

It was a silly idea and this place should probably be torn down in short order. Sadly, it wasn't the worst of the outbuildings he'd seen.

"Let's go have a look at the building midway between here and the gatehouse. The one that has a slag heap in the yard."

"It's not a slag heap, it's going to be our mill as soon as I have enough money to get it back in operation," Mary said as they began heading down the freshly graveled path.

Her breath came in little white puffs as she described her plans for the mill. A married couple named Sarah and Socrates Park had already moved into the small living area attached to the ground floor of the mill, but it would be at least a year before she could get the waterwheel back in operation.

He said nothing as they continued walking, but it annoyed him that she would move people into the millhouse before they were ready to go into operation.

"Please tell me you aren't paying these people a salary," he said.

"Of course not!"

"Then how are they supporting themselves?"

Mary trudged forward, a hint of defensiveness in her tone. "I let them live rent free. They're making pottery until I can get the mill working. They've set up quite an operation in the yard, which you mistook for a slag heap."

It *was* a slag heap. Dozens of terracotta urns were stacked up, ready to be glazed. Shelves weighed down with smaller pieces looked out of place in the yard. Broken bits of pottery and a wobbly worktable littered the muddy patch of land that was barren of grass. An anemic trickle of water barely moved in the stream alongside the mill.

"I usually give the Parks advance notice before I visit," Mary said, a hint of unease in her voice. "Wait here."

She scurried to the opposite side of the mill, but he followed. What did she intend to hide? Whatever it was, the tension drained from her face by the time he joined her and could see through the double doors pulled wide open. The

doors were built to accommodate wagonloads of grain enter-
ing and leaving the interior of the mill. A few millstones and
a drive shaft were propped against the wall, but most of the
space had been given over to worktables, pottery wheels, and
paint supplies. A rumpled bed and kitchen area must be where
the couple was living.

Mary picked up a glazed bowl, turning it so he could see
the pattern of forget-me-not flowers bordering the rim.

"See?" she said. "The forget-me-not pattern is Sarah's
design and very popular in town. People love it."

Mary went on to explain that the Parks had probably gone
into town to make a delivery to the local shops, for they always
did good business at Christmas.

If business was so good, she ought to be charging them
rent. It looked like the Parks were taking full advantage of the
space, but he would rather discuss the milling operation.

"What are your plans for getting the mill running again?"

"I plan on dredging the stream next summer," Mary said.
"Socrates Park is a miller by trade, but they love making pottery. There's no harm in letting them do it until I can pay for
the renovation."

"When was the last time this mill was used?" he asked.

"It was when my great-grandfather was alive, so at least
eighty years ago."

The past eighty years had seen a revolution in industrial-
ization, and there might not be any point in trying to adapt
this relic to serve as a modern milling operation. It would
require a qualified engineer to install new gears, axel, and
grinding mechanisms, but it wasn't something he could
accomplish on this trip.

"Tell me about the gatehouse," he said as he started back

down the path. Given the handsome structure and location near the road, he certainly hoped she was charging a premium rental price.

"The Papadakis brothers live there," she said. "Three brothers. They're musicians from Greece, and what a terribly sad story they have. They came to England last year to claim an inheritance, but it turned out that the bulk of the estate had been invested in a Canadian railroad scheme. The inheritance proved worthless by the time they arrived to claim it, and they had no money for the trip back to Greece. They're stranded here and have been with me ever since. They are musicians, and I do enjoy hearing them play on warm summer evenings."

A niggling suspicion took root, and he prayed it wasn't true but kept his voice carefully neutral. "And how much are you charging them to lease the gatehouse?"

"Well! It was in bad repair when they arrived. I wouldn't feel comfortable charging them anything," she said defensively.

"It's a habitable structure."

"It is *now*, but you should have seen it when they arrived. They patched the roof and painted the exterior. It was a lot of work that I couldn't tackle."

He quickened his steps, for the gatehouse was straight ahead. Built mostly of old red brick, it was a charming building with spacious wings framing the large tunnel through which his carriage passed yesterday. The brothers hadn't done much. The patched roof looked shabby and since most of the building was brick, there hadn't even been much to paint, and yet the brothers continued to enjoy rent-free living.

He strode to the front door and knocked. Mary scurried up beside him. "They don't really speak English," she said.

"Then how did you learn their sob story?"

"Well, the oldest brother speaks a little English, but not much. I also got details from their grandfather's lawyer in town. Please don't be angry. And you shouldn't knock so loud; they're probably still asleep."

At nine o'clock in the morning? He hadn't slept in this late since the time he had pneumonia as a teenager. He knocked louder, and at last there were sounds of life stirring inside. Fumbling, shuffling, coughing. The door finally opened and a tousle-haired young man, bathrobe hanging open, rubbed the sleep from his eyes, but smiled when he saw Mary.

"Maria!" he bellowed joyously, flinging his arms wide and stepping outside to embrace Mary, even though he had bare feet and practically no clothes. He gave her a kiss on both cheeks and a rambling monologue in a language Everett couldn't understand. Mary seemed to bask in the attention, especially when another brother appeared a moment later. More embracing, more rambling spiels in Greek.

They certainly weren't shy. They ushered Mary inside and held the door for him as well. Inside was appalling. Unwashed dishes and half-empty bottles cluttered the tables. Clothes were draped over every available piece of furniture. A violin lay abandoned on the floor and a cello was propped in the corner. Several other stringed instruments were balanced atop mounds of dirty clothes.

Another man lay dozing on a small settee, although he opened a bleary eye and rolled upright when he saw Mary. The men were obviously related… all of them with similar curling black hair and handsome faces.

"Who here speaks English?" he asked.

There was a long pause during which a cat slinked forward and Mary squatted to scoop it up. The three brothers exchanged glances, and finally the one on the settee pushed himself to his feet, pulled on a battered old soldier's jacket, and offered his hand.

"Marco," he said, then made a pinching gesture with his hand. "Little bit English."

"Tell your brothers I intend to start charging 'little bit rent' for this gatehouse. Ten shillings a month, beginning in January."

"You can't do that!" Mary gasped.

"Why not?" He kept his gaze darting among the brothers. They didn't say anything, but given the transformation on all three faces, they understood what he just said and didn't like it.

"They don't have any form of income. They're musicians," she said. "Everyone knows musicians are poor. It comes with the territory."

"Yes," one of the brothers said before Marco nudged him and sent a silencing glare.

"It costs me nothing to let them live here," Mary said. "They buy their own food and fuel. And I like having them here. Where's the harm?"

The harm was that this estate seemed to be supporting a camp of vagrant nomads, and that wasn't the image he wanted for Whitefriars. At least the Papadakis brothers kept their squalor confined to the interior of the building, not scattered all over the yard like the potters.

Leasing the tower room was bad enough, but housing a collection of misfits in the outbuildings seemed to be her objective. She actually *liked* having these outsiders here. It wouldn't get any better unless he reined her in.

"Let's head outside." He shot a surly glare at Marco. "You and I will discuss this later," he said before leaving. It was appalling that Mary let herself be used like this, and he intended to put an end to it.

CHAPTER FIVE

MARY FOLLOWED EVERETT outside, scrambling for a way to defuse his anger. The Papadakis brothers brought a flash of warmth into her world with their endlessly cheerful presence. It didn't matter that she hadn't been able to converse much, or that they'd been taking advantage of her benevolence, she needed them here. The Parks, too. Socrates and Sarah Park weren't nearly as much fun, but they were solid and dependable and because of their age they almost felt like a second set of parents.

It was hard to keep up with Everett's stride, and the cold air winded her. "Slow down," she urged as they crossed the stone bridge spanning the creek.

Everett whirled to face her. "Everything I've seen at Whitefriars is unacceptable. Completely unfit for paying guests. The shabby outbuildings, the inadequate heat, the substandard food, the—"

"Our food isn't substandard!"

He snorted. "The dinner last night featured muffins that didn't rise properly and the fish was overbaked. The Whitefriars name implies culinary excellence. Any paying guest has a right to expect as much instead of bland meals from a mediocre cook."

She blanched. Mrs. Galloway had been their cook ever since Mary could remember. True, the meals at Whitefriars leaned toward the country cooking that was hearty and filling rather than delicate and refined, but she loved Mrs. Galloway. It was Mrs. Galloway who used to bandage her skinned knees and who comforted her the one and only time she'd had a beau. When Jerome Zaxby decided life in London suited him better than a crumbling country estate, it was Mrs. Galloway who listened to Mary's heartsick ramblings. When the estate was at its worst and the ceiling in the music room caved in during a rainstorm, Mrs. Galloway worked beside her through that awful night emptying buckets and helping salvage the eighteenth-century tapestries.

"Don't you dare say anything bad about Mrs. Galloway," she warned.

"I'm sure she's a fine woman, but she's not a fine cook," he snapped, his blue eyes unbelievably cold and hard. "She can't deliver the quality a guest would have a right to expect if they come to the house that is the symbolic image of my entire company."

She looked away from his critical scrutiny, landing on the beloved warm stones of the castle. Seeing it through Everett's eyes hurt, for the grounds *were* shabby. And maybe the food wasn't as fine as that served at the Knightsbridge Inn, but no one ever complained. She'd spent the last nine years struggling to restore this place, and yet how quickly he belittled it. She waited the entire year for Christmas when she could share Whitefriars with her family, and all Everett had done was ruin it.

"I think you're being very judgmental," she said, but he continued his rant as though he hadn't heard.

"You're squandering an asset," he said. "These outbuildings should be profitably deployed or torn down and turned into a garden that would enhance the value of the estate. Whitefriars has the potential to be a model of innovative restoration, and yet you're doing nothing with it other than collecting a band of misfits."

It felt like a slap. It took every ounce of fortitude not to run away, but she forced herself to meet his eyes and speak calmly. "Maybe I'm a misfit, too."

That took him aback. For the first time a little starch went out of him and he shifted uneasily. "You're not a misfit," he said.

"What was I doing the first time you saw me?" She was doubled over and on the verge of fainting from nothing more threatening than being away from Whitefriars. He'd treated her decently, but he'd seen her howling weakness.

"That doesn't make you a misfit," he denied.

Chronic agoraphobia didn't exactly lend itself to a London season or being able to form proper friendships. Instead, she cared for the graves of long-dead monks and daydreamed about the people who lived here centuries ago. There wasn't any point in arguing about this, but she needed to make one thing blindingly clear.

"I don't care what you think about me, and feel free to look down your nose at the Papadakis brothers, but don't you dare insult Mrs. Galloway. That woman was more of a mother to me than my real one, and if you hurt her feelings, I'll come after you with torches and a pitchfork."

She strode toward the castle, wishing her legs were longer

so she could outdistance him, but he kept apace with her. At least he was quiet. If he said one more insulting statement about Whitefriars she'd combust.

Nick was leading a saddled horse out of the stables as she arrived. He sent them a good-natured wave as they approached, but she was in no mood for it. Nick was always so cheerful, and right now she wanted to burn something down.

"Wish me luck," Nick said as he mounted. "I'm heading into the village to see if I can find something for dinner. What the cook planned isn't panning out so well."

The stress Mrs. Galloway had been put through all so that Everett could enjoy blue food twisted her anger even higher. Couldn't he understand how hard they'd been trying to please him? Instead, all he could do was insult her home, her cook, and her tenants.

"What had the cook planned?" Everett asked.

"Some sort of clotted cream sauce. Since white food is no longer mandatory, I'm out in search of something a little heartier." Humor danced in Nick's dark eyes, and maybe he thought this was all a joke, but she was still teetering on the edge of a precipice all because of Everett Wooten's unexpected visit and irrational standards.

To her surprise, Everett asked to accompany Nick, who readily agreed. It didn't take long to saddle another horse and Mary watched as the two men rode away. The village was only two miles down the road, but it felt as if a weight had been lifted from her chest as she returned to the house.

She paused outside the front door, laying her palm over the thick mahogany wood. Castle records indicated this door dated from the seventeenth century. It was embellished with hand-forged strap hinges that each featured the shape of a roaring lion's head at the end. How she used to gawk at those whimsical lions as a child, even though they'd been crusted over with rust and the wood had been damaged. She'd rubbed her hands raw restoring this door, oiling the wood, buffing away the rust, and paying a master blacksmith more than she could afford to mend the hardware. This door was now as handsome as it had been when first installed hundreds of years ago. She pressed her forehead to the door, sending up a prayer.

Dear Lord, what is it you want of me? I've tried to be a good steward to this estate, but it seems I am failing.

She hadn't comported herself well today. She'd been short-tempered and defensive, acting on instinct to protect Whitefriars.

So is Everett.

Where had that thought come from? It was a strange thought, but in his own way Everett wanted good things for Whitefriars, too. It wasn't from any love for the history of the place, it was all about his food company, but over the years he had been consistently helpful to her. For nine years they had been exchanging letters, and he never failed her a single time.

"I shall do better," she vowed. In Galatians, Paul advised *let us not grow weary of doing good, for in due season we will reap, if we do not give up.*

"Mary? Are you all right?" She pulled back from the door, embarrassed to be caught praying on the front porch as Rosalind opened the door, concern on her gentle face.

"I'm fine," she said.

Rosalind was such an accomplished woman. She'd travelled all over the world, spoke foreign languages, and had a doctorate in biochemistry. Mary felt so paltry in comparison, a woman who couldn't even bring herself to leave Whitefriars without risking a debilitating attack of panic.

"I saw you and Mr. Wooten walking down by the mill. Has he been helpful?"

He'd been a nightmare, but Mary swallowed back the unkind thoughts. "He pointed out some things that need attention."

She must not grow weary of trying to do her best. Eventually Whitefriars would be good enough to please even someone of Everett Wooten's exacting standards.

***

An hour later Mary hurried to the watermill, anxious to speak with Socrates Park about the state of the mill. Socrates was the man she'd hired to help get the mill back in working order and there hadn't been much progress on that front. An engineer by training, he knew the mechanics of rotating mills, but he and his wife seemed to prefer the artistry of a pottery wheel instead.

She'd gotten used to the unkempt yard surrounding the mill, but Everett was right. It looked a mess. The Parks could at least tidy up the yard. Their wagon was back, so they'd returned from town, but the wide sliding doors had been pulled shut and the draperies closed over the windows. Paying an unexpected visit to the Parks was never a good idea. She cocked her ear to listen but heard nothing.

"Mr. Park?" she asked, knocking loudly. "Mr. Park, are you home?"

There was some thudding from inside, then a squeal and scraping sound. "One moment," Socrates called out, his voice muffled. She withdrew a few yards and waited while more scrambling sounds came from inside. The Parks were middle-aged people, but they'd found each other late in life. Socrates was in his mid-fifties and his wife only a few years younger. Unannounced visits always carried the potential for embarrassment.

One of the double doors pulled open a few inches, revealing Socrates and his wild mane of salt-and-pepper hair, his face flushed with good cheer.

"Hello, Mary," he said. "Nice to see you."

She drew her cloak tighter. "It's freezing out here. Can I come in?"

Socrates glanced behind him, keeping most of the opening blocked.

"She can come in," Sarah called out. Mary wouldn't mind remaining out here a few moments longer, just to be certain all was in order, but Socrates pulled the door wide and tugged her inside. As expected, Sarah was adjusting her bodice and her fading auburn hair tumbled down her back in glorious disarray.

"What brings you here on this fine day?" Socrates asked.

"Don't be rude, offer her something to drink," Sarah said, then reached for a shawl to wrap around her shoulders.

Socrates darted across the modest living area to the small kitchen with a stove, cooking pans hanging from hooks, and shelves weighed down with Sarah's handmade crockery. He eyed the offerings on the bottom shelf. "Tea? Warm milk? Hot cocoa?"

She shook her head, for there was nothing cozy about her need to speak with them. "I came to see if you have an estimate for when the watermill might be back in operation."

Sarah looked concerned as she pulled her shawl tighter, and Socrates rubbed his jaw, the good cheer of moments ago having fled.

"It might be a while," he said uneasily. "The drive shaft needs to be replaced and it will need a new grain hopper and sluice gate. That's a lot of work. Expensive work, too."

No doubt. It would probably take years to recoup the investment and she didn't mind letting the Parks use the space as a pottery studio. But Everett did, and he had the power of that contract.

"Can you make a list of what still needs to be done, and estimate the costs?" Perhaps if modernizing the mill was too expensive Everett would lose interest.

"I suppose. Why the sudden urgency?"

"You know the American investor who helped with financing the castle renovation?"

Socrates nodded.

"He's here, and he is very concerned with the estate turning a profit."

Understanding dawned on Socrates's face. "Oh," he grumbled. "Americans."

She tried to smile. "Yes. Americans."

She pulled her cloak tighter, wondering how her entire world turned off-kilter so quickly. It had been only a few days ago when Everett barged into her safe, contained world. Socrates laid a large, work-roughened palm on her shoulder, his face drawn in concern.

"Is he giving you a hard time?"

His kindness got to her. From the day Socrates moved here, he had been looking out for her. He'd been a hero in helping maintain the drainage lines in the east field, and when her dog died last spring she sensed he was the only person who really understood. A lot of people didn't appreciate how a mangy old terrier could feel like a best friend. Colin kept saying she should simply get another dog, but she was still mourning and wasn't ready yet. Socrates understood, and for that she was grateful.

"No, Everett is all right," she said. "I think if you can present a timetable for the mill improvements it might satisfy him. At least for now. In the meantime, can you and Sarah tidy up the yard? He's quite particular about appearances."

Socrates nodded. "I suppose we can do that right now."

"I'll help." She didn't want to admit it, but she didn't quite trust the Parks' standards in terms of tidiness. Besides, she didn't want Sarah overdoing things.

Mary learned about Sarah's condition shortly after they moved in. Most days Sarah was vibrant and cheerful, but on occasion her heart simply started to fail, leaving her weak and blue around the lips.

Mary panicked the first time she saw it. Sarah had been carrying a tray of newly fired pottery when she dropped the load and staggered to sit atop an overturned barrel. Socrates hunkered down beside her, rubbing her hands but remarkably calm.

Mary wanted to run for a doctor, but Sarah dissuaded her. "There's nothing a doctor can do," Sarah said faintly. "I was born this way, and I've always known my life would be shorter than most. The doctor says I've lived with this condition longer than anyone he's ever seen. Socrates knew but married me anyway."

"And never regretted it," her husband had said, squeezing her hand. His eyes looked a little watery, but he still managed a smile as he turned to Mary. "It's why we never waste a day. Not an hour. Life is short, and we celebrate the time we have every day."

That had been two years ago, and it was one of the reasons Mary never begrudged the blatant physical affection the two indulged.

Three hours later the yard looked better. She and Socrates did the heavy lifting in clearing the yard while Sarah collected the broken pottery that could be reused to make new slurry. Unfired pottery was collected into crates and moved inside. It was hard to make the muddy, barren yard look presentable, but the refuse was gone and it might pass muster with Everett.

The fragile sense of hope remained all the way until she entered through the front door of the castle and saw Nick on the front steps with Colin, recounting what had happened with Everett in the village.

***

"You should have seen him!" Nick boomed. "Everett moved through the marketplace like a general inspecting the troops, firing off questions to the vendors and buying things left, right, and center."

"Things? What things?" Mary asked.

"Chickens, little bottles of fancy vinegar, a million types of herbs, and something called risotto, whatever that is. He bought two wheels of imported cheese that cost more than most people earn in a week. Honestly, I've never seen a man attack a market with such zeal. He's in the kitchen with Mrs.

Galloway now. Poor woman looked like he was speaking a foreign language when he started giving her instructions."

A lead weight dropped into her stomach. He'd better not be expecting Mrs. Galloway to know what to do with all these fancy ingredients. If he wanted a gourmet meal, he could turn around and be at the Knightsbridge Inn before dinner. Nick was still gushing over Everett's culinary excess, but she darted down the corridor to rescue Mrs. Galloway.

And Mrs. Galloway needed it. The farm table was filled with sacks, bottles, wheels of cheese, and eight dead chickens. Everett held a jug of cream and spoke calmly to a frazzled Mrs. Galloway.

"Crème fraiche isn't difficult, but you mustn't heat it too quickly," he said. "And the correct amount of buttermilk is imperative if you are to coax the bacterial cultures into proper fermentation."

Oh, dear heaven, Mrs. Galloway needed recuing immediately! Mary summoned her most authoritative voice to nip this madness in the bud.

"We don't make crème fraiche in this household," she said. She had no idea what crème fraiche was, but if it involved fermentation and bacterial cultures it was beyond what their kitchen could produce.

Everett quirked a brow, but Mrs. Galloway looked befuddled. "We don't? I've never heard of it, but it doesn't seem too difficult. I'm willing to try."

Everett nodded in approval. "You'll find that it is the perfect accompaniment for a roasted chicken. It's a wonderful, rich, custard of a cream with complex flavors despite the simplicity of the ingredients. I'll walk you through it."

This was exactly what she feared. Everett was setting Mrs.

Galloway up for failure but she wouldn't let it happen. She crossed the kitchen to grab an apron hanging on a hook beside the work counter.

"I'll help," she said. She didn't know much about cooking but wouldn't leave Mrs. Galloway alone to be humiliated by their unwelcome visitor.

CHAPTER SIX

EVERETT RECOGNIZED THE fighting spirit in Mary as she donned the apron, but he wouldn't let that dim his afternoon. For the first time in weeks he'd have a chance to revel in the production of a grand, pull-out-the-stops culinary masterpiece. If Whitefriars was to offer rooms for lease, they would need to live up to the name on every jar of gourmet jam, sauce, and seasoned vinegar he sold.

Besides, he liked cooking and it had been weeks since he'd been able to indulge his secret vice.

"Can you pluck a chicken?" he asked Mary.

She blanched, swiveling her elegant head to stare in trepidation at the mound of dead chickens on the worktable. It was a struggle to keep the laughter from his face, but Mrs. Galloway interrupted the fun by rushing to the rescue.

"I can pluck the chickens," she said, dropping the whisk and stepping away from the stove.

"Keep stirring," he urged. "If the cream rises above eighty-five degrees it can curdle."

Mrs. Galloway looked torn but obeyed. With no salvation

on the horizon, Mary took a step toward the chickens, reaching a hand out to pinch a leathery claw and drag the first bird a little closer. She was going to do it! His admiration soared, but he needed those chickens plucked in short order, and it would take a beginner forever. And Mary was clearly a beginner. Her face was frozen in mortification and she was holding her breath, but she grasped a few feathers and tugged.

"Stop," he said. "You've got three healthy young men living the life of Riley in the gatehouse. They don't need to speak English to pluck chickens." Even though he was convinced they *did* speak English. Mary was too kind-hearted and willing to see the best in people. Maybe he was the opposite. He and his father hadn't risen to the top of the packaged food industry by letting people live rent free or make pottery when they'd been hired to mill wheat.

Nick could run the chickens down to the Papadakis brothers, for unlike Mary, the burly former plumber would have no problem reading the riot act to the brothers. The look of relief on her face when he suggested Nick take the chickens down to the brothers was comical and she dashed out of the kitchen to fetch him.

Ten minutes later Nick had taken the chickens away and Mary's expression looked brighter. "What can I do to help?"

It was impressive how she could still sound so elegant and refined, her head held high on that swan-like neck as she waited for instructions.

"I could use the carrots and potatoes washed and chopped," he said. "The menu tonight is roasted chicken with vegetables and a crème fraiche dressing, mushroom risotto with wine sauce. I'm not sure about dessert yet."

By heaven, he loved cooking. Aside from business, it was

the only thing he was truly good at. And since he didn't particularly enjoy the business side of his life, these rare moments in the kitchen were too few and precious to squander.

"What now?" Mrs. Galloway asked, for the buttermilk and heavy cream had reached the right temperature. He guided her through the next steps, all under Mary's watchful gaze. Did Mary think he was going to belittle Mrs. Galloway?

It was a ridiculous thought. The old cook reminded him of Yvonne, the French woman who cooked for their family all his life. Yvonne taught him how to whisk a sauce, season a roast, select a blend of sweet and tart for the ultimate in desserts. While other boys and young men played sports, chased skirts, or tromped through fields in a pointless quest to hunt innocent birds, he learned how to cook. And he loved every moment of it.

Their family hadn't started out in the food business. His father had been a poor kid from Brooklyn who started life as a shoe salesman. Then Frank Wooten developed a successful shoe polish, packaged it, and made a healthy return. Then he used the same packaging technique for whale oil and made a bigger return. By the time Everett was born his father was one of the richest men in New York, canning and tinning any number of industrial products.

New York was home to high-society millionaires, many of them self-made. They bought country estates, married impoverished daughters of dukes, and aped European aristocracy. That had never been Frank Wooten's concern. As a boy who had known hunger growing up, Frank merely wanted to make money, and he'd been good at it. He patented a method of vacuum sealing jars that could preserve products indefinitely, whether it was whale oil, shoe polish, or a particularly delicious recipe of sweet and tart berries made in his own kitchen.

His father was smart. Instead of mass producing his jam, he partnered with Colin Beckwith, an impoverished aristocrat who had a title, a castle, and the perfect branding for creating an overpriced luxury line of food.

His father soon turned the food line over to Everett. Once he had control, Everett created an entire line of gourmet sauces and jams unlike anything on the American market. He and Yvonne tested hundreds of recipes. After their success with the jam, they created a sweet and spicy line of mustards. He created a smoky fig and garlic spread, then a caramelized and balsamic onion sauce that was secretly being used at all the finest restaurants in Manhattan. After Whitefriars Gourmet conquered the East Coast he signed deals to release it in Europe, Latin America, even Russia. He built a fortune from the Whitefriars line, and no one even knew that he had personally created all the recipes.

Mary made quick work of the vegetables, so he set her to preparing the glaze. It would be an ambitious one, but he'd help her with it. Pouring some mustard seeds into a mortar, he showed her how to grind them into a powder.

"Once the mustard is ground, we'll use honey and the raspberry vinegar to add some sweetness, along with a bit of ginger for spice."

Mary and Mrs. Galloway both gaped at him as though he'd lost his head. It was hard not to smile. "You need to trust me on this. Mrs. Galloway, are there any fresh lemons in the house?"

She nodded. "I keep them jarred and salted to last the winter."

"Excellent! A bit of lemon juice and grated rind will brighten the entire dish. Fetch the lemons!"

The kitchen filled with scents of herbs and citrus as he whisked sauces, simmered preserves, and began heating vegetables. Nick returned with the freshly plucked chickens, reporting that the Papadakis brothers put up only minimal resistance. After a stern lecture in Greek by the older brother, all three men got to work and had the chickens plucked in short order.

Everett rubbed a combination of herbs and spices onto the chicken skin, added the vegetables, then set it all in the oven to roast.

"That seemed so easy," Mary said as he closed the oven door, looking around for something else to do.

"Baste them with the pan juices every fifteen minutes until they're finished," he advised. In the meantime, he set her to grating parmesan cheese, mincing garlic, and chopping shallots as he showed Mrs. Galloway how to make the risotto sauce.

Over the next hour the most amazing thing happened. Aromas from the kitchen beckoned others inside. Dinner wouldn't be ready for over an hour, but first Colin and Lucy drifted inside, each nursing a pre-dinner cordial, then Nick and Rosalind came as well. It was amazing the way Mary lit up with their arrival, refilling their glasses and laughing over the stories they told about their children.

Cooking was second nature to him, so it was easy to keep cooking while paying attention to Mary, fascinated by how she chatted with people so effortlessly. Her first question was always about the other person, not the business at hand. Sometimes she even laid an encouraging hand on their forearm while she spoke. People simply seemed to light up when Mary was near. He certainly did. He could learn from her. He'd always been a disaster at conversation, but she made it seem easy.

The dough that had been rising was probably ready to be divided and shaped into baguettes. He folded the dough, flipped, turned, and pressed it again, gradually shaping it into the classic French baguette. They hadn't had time to bake something for dessert, but a pan of dried-out blueberry vanilla cake had been left over from the disastrous blue tea, and he would figure out a way to rescue it. Tipping cocoa powder into a pan of cream, he whisked until it was a glossy, chocolatey sauce filling the kitchen with its sweetly divine scent. Then he reached for the small bottle purchased at the market today.

"No way," Nick hollered from the other side of the kitchen. "You are *not* adding soy sauce to chocolate."

"Watch me," he said, splashing a generous swirl into the mix. Howls of protest came from the opposite side of the kitchen, but what did these people know about cooking? He'd been eating from this kitchen for two days, and it was obvious their standards were subpar.

He might not find chatting and small talk easy, but he knew his way around a kitchen.

***

While the others eventually lost interest in the cooking and left for the great hall, Mary continued helping Everett. She sliced the baguettes and topped them with a smoky fig and caramelized onion seasoning Everett prepared, then popped them back into the oven once more. What an amazing bounty of food! They filled serving bowls, baskets, and platters, laying it all out on the oversized sideboard. The chickens were roasted alongside carrots, russet potatoes, and leeks. The mushroom risotto was a blend of white cream sauce speckled with chives and mushrooms. Even the dessert was colorful, a blueberry vanilla cake and a glossy chocolate glaze.

"It's a bounty of colors," she teased Everett. "Not a white meal at all."

Was it possible he was actually blushing? He was clearly trying to block a smile as he spoke. "I only do the food bet for a single week each month. Tomorrow I will telegram my father to let him know he won this month."

This was good, Mary silently thought. Everything was good tonight, for during the hours while they'd been cooking, the ice had broken. They were friends again. Surely he would not assert that hideous clause in the contract now that they were so friendly.

She got down seven plates from the shelf, for it seemed only right to ask Mrs. Galloway to join them at the table since she ought to be able to taste the bounty, too. They weren't formal here, so everyone would serve themselves and carry their own plates into the corner of the great hall that served as a dining room. She was about to summon the others when Nick came striding into the kitchen.

"Those Greek brothers are here," he said. "They're carry-ing a bunch of instruments, and as near as I can tell, they are offering to play for us during dinner."

She drew in an alarmed breath. The fastest thing to stoke Everett's suspicions again would be to remind him of how the

Papadakis brothers had been exploiting her generosity. Everett was right and she needed to do something about them, but not tonight.

"Tell them we don't need music," she said, for she knew what would happen if they stayed. They would play a little music, then invite themselves to dinner. They'd done it every time they ever offered to play, and in the past she'd been glad of their company. They were always so relentlessly cheerful and fun, even if she couldn't understand a word they said. How much did you need to understand when they balanced a jug on their nose or built towers with the dinner rolls? It would be a disaster to let Everett see them at their worst.

"We don't have enough to feed them," she said, her spirit sagging as she eyed the bounty weighing down the sideboard. They had enough food for days. Before she could think of a better excuse, Colin sauntered into the kitchen with Lucy and Rosalind right behind.

"Music?" Colin said. "What a fine idea! One of those fellows has a mandolin. It will remind me of my summer in Corfu."

"Please say yes!" Lucy added. "Perhaps they can play Christmas carols. One of them was already plucking out 'God Rest Ye Merry Gentlemen' on his violin."

"Do you suppose they know 'Angels We Have Heard on High'?" Rosalind asked. "That's always been my favorite. And can they sing, too?"

"Not in English," she said. Already she noticed Everett's downturned mouth, his darkening expression.

"I'll bet they can sing in six different languages, including English," Everett muttered as he tipped the last of the risotto into a serving dish.

"Go tell them to join us," Colin said. "Better yet, send someone for the Parks, too. Let's make a feast of it!"

The Parks weren't as bad as the Papadakis brothers. She could depend on the fact that they wouldn't drink too much or start playing toss with the antique candlesticks, but she wasn't any good at saying no to people. She looked helplessly at Everett.

"You're the guest of honor," she said. "And the cook, too. You get to make the call. I'm sure Colin will respect your decision."

Please, please, please tell the brothers to go home, she silently implored. Everett seemed too strait-laced to welcome the rambunctious guests to his culinary feast. His brows lowered as he scanned the meal set out on the sideboard, a look of fierce concentration on his face. She held her breath, waiting for his verdict.

"I've done a lot of bold experimentation with the flavors tonight," he said. "I'd like as many opinions as possible."

"Bring in the brothers and send for the Parks!" Colin hollered to Nick, who was already bounding down the hall to welcome the brothers inside.

This was going to be a disaster.

CHAPTER SEVEN

THE GREAT HALL featured a long dining table only a few yards from the fireplace. It was the grandest room in the castle, but the laughter from those gathered around the table made it seem cozy.

Everett didn't consider tonight's dinner to be a feast, it was an experiment. Although everyone else ate, laughed, and sang along with the Christmas carols, he paid careful attention to how each person responded to the meal. He watched their expressions, observed how quickly they ate, and noticed which dishes did not get finished.

He was most interested in the children's reactions. Nick's oldest daughter was seven and Colin had a three-year-old. Most children that young didn't care for the complex flavors in the sauces served tonight, and indeed, the toddler screwed up her little face in distaste at the pungent chicken, but she seemed to like the creamy risotto. He'd improvised the seasoning for the chicken, but it could easily be bottled and sold if it had enough appeal.

At one point the brothers set their instruments down and joined them at the table, filling their plates high. He was curious to see how people from the Mediterranean liked the flavors, for he was expanding their sales throughout Europe and some cultures didn't care for the seasonings he used tonight.

"What do you think of the flavor of the chicken?" he asked the oldest Papadakis brother.

Marco hesitated and glanced at Mary for a moment before answering, surely concerned with keeping their supposed inability to speak English alive. "Good," he finally said. "Good chicken."

"It was marvelous," Rosalind said. "What a treat it is to have you cook for us."

"Now that your secret is out we shall keep you locked in the kitchen," Nick said.

"Better yet, he can come cook for us at the mill!" Socrates said, his wife snuggled alongside him in an unseemly display of affection.

Everett accepted the compliments with a polite nod, but he preferred to keep his ability to cook quiet. He'd rather the world see him as a man of business. His gaze trailed to Mary, who was leaning in to hear soft-spoken Rosalind over the rousing laughter of the men. Her face was animated and alive, her eyes sparkling in the candlelight. One of the children toddled over to her and begged to be picked up. Mary obliged, bouncing the child on her knee while continuing to talk to Rosalind.

How easily she mingled and chatted with everyone. Normally he didn't feel comfortable with such exuberant people, but from the moment they met he enjoyed everything about her. The companionship, her curiosity, watching her take joy in everything from tending the monks' graves to mingling with the rowdy Papadakis brothers.

And yet… and yet.

She rarely left this place. She panicked when she did. She considered herself a misfit.

Very odd.

A wild, masculine groan of appreciation interrupted his thoughts. The youngest Papadakis brother, a man whose handsome good looks probably allowed him to get away with far too much in life, was sprawled in his chair, head thrown back, moaning as he savored the chocolate sauce. He sat up for another bite, then repeated the overblown moan and rambled something in Greek.

"Theo says very good chocolate," Marco translated.

Daydreaming about Mary made him forgetful about monitoring people's reactions. The soy sauce. It was the secret weapon to make a delicious chocolate sauce border on divine. He slanted a knowing look at Nick. "What did I tell you?"

Nick held up his hands. "I give up. It was good."

"As soon as Theo rejoins us back on earth, perhaps we can have some more Christmas carols?" Colin asked.

Theo was reluctantly parted from the chocolate, then picked up his cello and bow. The others reached for their violins.

Marco asked in broken English what they'd like to hear. So far, they'd been playing mostly traditional Christmas songs.

"You choose," Colin said.

The brothers conferred in Greek, with Theo arguing vehemently about something. Finally, a tune was selected, and they took their positions.

"We write this song ourselves," Marco said.

"You wrote the song?" Mary asked.

Marco nodded. "Yes. This week we write the song." He

nodded to the others, they lifted their instruments, waited a moment, and then the tune began.

Rich, warm notes filled the hall. Out of nowhere a melodic harmony filled the air, but then came Theo's cello with its sorrowful notes, carrying a longing and a hunger, an unmistakable tune of mourning and grief. Then Marco's violin overlay the cello, reaching high and soaring with an intense cascade of notes that captured pure mastery of the instrument. It was alternately joyful and heartbreaking.

Everett leaned in closer, spellbound. The weight of the music, the heft, the unabashed emotionalism… it was magical. Everyone grew still as the music unrolled and wove a spell in the old castle. The three brothers took turns leading the tune, but all of them played together in a masterful dance of harmony and layers of sound.

When it was over, Everett sat motionless, astounded at what he'd just heard. What he knew about music could fit into a thimble, but this was the most profound music he'd heard in his life. Mary dabbed tears from her eyes, and everyone was moved.

Theo set his cello aside, stood up, and faced Marco. He unleashed a rush of Greek words, his urgent tone breaking the mood with its angry torrent. Marco interrupted him, irritation in his voice. Soon all three brothers were yelling, pushing, and shoving. The middle brother, Flavian, seemed to be the peacemaker, trying to keep the oldest and youngest brother from attacking each other.

Were they really on the verge of a fight? After the majesty of the music they just played? Theo seemed the most passionate, thumping on his chest as he yelled at Marco. Tears started to flow down the younger man's face as anger twisted his words. When he drew back a fist, Flavian dove in to stop him, wrapping his arms around Theo, walking him back from their older brother. Then Theo started bawling, wailing out his grief while continuing to babble in Greek.

Marco turned to face them. "I am sorry. We go now."

He collected the instruments, while Flavian kept Theo restrained a few steps away. Soon Theo gave a nod of resignation, was released, and picked up his cello to follow his older brother out.

"I wonder what that was all about?" Mary asked once they were gone, looking baffled at how quickly the evening had collapsed.

"They're arguing about a girl back home," Rosalind said. "My Greek isn't strong, but I understood enough to know that Theo is in love with someone and wants to go back, but Marco said they have it good here. He won't leave."

"Oh dear," Mary said, wrapping her arms around herself. Was she frightened? She looked scared, but that didn't make any sense. Why should she care if three freeloading men left?

"Perhaps we could send for the girl?" Mary asked. "Would that make Theo feel better about staying?"

"Why would you do that?" Colin asked. It was a relief to hear a voice of reason challenging Mary's overly generous heart.

"Because I don't want them to leave," she said defensively. "I like having them here. I want them to stay."

"They don't pay any rent," Colin said pointedly.

Everett glanced at the Parks, who suddenly looked distinctly uncomfortable. Mary noticed too and sent them a reassuring glance before turning to face her brother.

"You left me here to manage this estate while you traipsed off to New York. It's my business who I invite to live here."

Colin stiffened. "I didn't exactly leave you destitute. I signed the deal with the Wootens. It's brought us good money over the years."

Mary's face reddened, and her hand clenched around her glass. "And I've appreciated it, but I have a life here and intend to live it as I choose. And if at all possible, I'd like the Papadakis brothers to stay."

Everett glanced between the two siblings. It wasn't the first time he'd noticed Mary's barbs directed at Colin, who'd mostly been absorbing them without retaliation. As much as Mary loved Whitefriars, she also resented her brother for leaving it.

***

Mary hated how quickly the gathering collapsed. The evening had begun so well, the sort of night she looked forward to all year. She was surrounded by family and friends, laughter and warmth. Maybe the brothers weren't truly friends since she couldn't even converse with them, but she still valued their company. And the Parks were almost like parents to her. And then of course, her in-laws from America, but they would be leaving soon and she'd be left by herself in a too-large house that was cold and lonely.

But after she unleashed her temper on Colin he went outside to smoke a cheroot and Lucy left because the children were fussy and needed to be put to bed. The Parks, looking chastened by the furious discussion of rent, left as soon as possible.

She did her best to salvage the evening by asking Rosalind how she learned Greek.

"I grew up in Germany," she said. "I had a very good

classical education, studying both Latin and Greek. I rarely have a chance to use it."

Once again, she felt small compared to Rosalind, who had so many accomplishments and experiences. Soon Rosalind and Nick left as well, leaving her alone with Everett, still sitting at the table, watching her with those thoughtful blue eyes.

"I'm sorry I spoiled your wonderful meal," she said.

He smiled tenderly. "You didn't spoil anything."

"It's my favorite season, and I ruined it! Christmas is the one time of year I get to be around family and I managed to annoy my only brother."

Everett's face was pensive as he scanned the room, trailing over the towering walls, the smoldering embers in the fireplace, and the wide, vacant space in the middle of the hall. "I can understand it must be lonely here. Have you ever thought of leaving?"

She paced around the table, drawing her shawl against a sudden shiver. "I could never leave here, even if I wanted."

"Because of the panic?"

She nodded. "Because of the panic. I feel so puny compared to Rosalind, who has sailed all over the world and accomplished so many things. And here I sit. Tending an old building."

"There's value in it."

The licensing deal. The image of the castle was on every jar of Whitefriars food. "Two thousand pounds a year," she said.

He caught the joke and laughed a little. "What I meant to say is, there is value in what you're doing here. I thought of something tonight while the brothers were playing."

She stiffened, praying he wouldn't reopen the argument, but he surprised her.

"As they were playing, I wondered if perhaps there is a reason they found their way to this estate, for the music we heard tonight was a gift from God. I've never heard anything so inspiring. In olden days, musicians were supported by patrons so they could have the time to create something very few people could accomplish. That was what we heard tonight, and you made it possible. You are their patron."

It was hard to breathe, because it was the greatest compliment she'd ever had in her life. How stunning for such extravagant praise to come from this most logical of men, but how she loved what he had just said. It made her feel worthy, like she belonged among the long line of caretakers who had looked after Whitefriars over the centuries.

She fought to keep the rush of emotion from her voice. "That may be the kindest thing anyone has ever said to me."

He was starting to soften, and she couldn't falter now. If only she could get him to see Whitefriars through her eyes, perhaps he would yield on that dreadful contract. Something inside her called to him. She needed longer to explore this new and wonderful connection to someone so different than she.

"Will you stay until Christmas?" she asked. "There is so much I can learn from you, and I'm not talking about chicken seasoning or chocolate sauces. You're not like anyone I've ever met. And I can show you the rest of the estate. You've only seen a fraction of it. Please say you'll stay."

She caught her breath at the expression on his face. His gaze clung to hers, filled with a blend of longing, hunger, and, strangely, a look of hope. It took effort not to fling herself into his arms. She was prepared to do almost anything to convince him to stay, but didn't need to.

"I'll stay," he said. "I'll be glad to stay."

CHAPTER EIGHT

EVERETT MIGHT COME to regret it, but he agreed to spend the entire Christmas week at Whitefriars. That meant he'd be here for five more days, trying to make conversation with strangers, rusticating in the wilderness, getting behind on business.

And falling in love with Mary Beckwith.

He never expected anything like this. His entire life had been an effort to avoid socializing with bright, bubbly people, but from the moment he met her there had been a magnetism between them.

But he couldn't abandon business entirely. His trip to Berlin needed to be delayed, and he needed to notify the company as soon as possible. First thing in the morning he followed the scent of freshly brewed tea and country bacon to the kitchen. Mary sat with Lucy and Rosalind, all three women nursing cups of tea and wearing thickly knitted shawls. Aside from Mary, he'd never been at ease around women and had been hoping to meet privately with Colin about wiring a message to Berlin. It would be rude to head back to the privacy of the tower room, so he put on a pleasant expression and joined them. He would follow Mary's example of initiating conversation by asking questions of the others.

"How did everyone sleep?" he asked.

It worked like a charm. Lucy pointed out that having an infant and a three-year-old precluded a good night's sleep, and Rosalind had plenty to say about wrestling with the feather-bed. This side of the castle had been completely renovated, so Mary and her family all had comfortable bedrooms, but Ever-ett was grateful for the privacy of the tower, even if it wasn't fully up to snuff yet.

"Was the fireplace able to keep the tower warm?" Mary asked.

"Much better," he said, which was true. Now that the fireplace was functioning it worked well enough to take the worst of the chill from the air.

He began filling his plate from the sideboard. Scrambled eggs, pickled herring, and fried potatoes. It was an ordinary breakfast, and he'd have to think of a way to elevate it should Mary's plan to lease the tower come to fruition.

"I was hoping to see Colin this morning," he said as he joined the others at the table.

"He and Nick went out hunting grouse," Mary said. "I don't know why he bothers. Colin refuses to actually shoot them, but he likes the challenge of finding them. He fires in the air to scare them into flight, then simply admires them as they fly away."

It seemed an odd way to waste time, especially since there was some urgency to his request. "Do you know when he'll return? I need to send a wire to Berlin."

Lucy perked up. "I can send a wire for you."

"You know Morse code?" he asked in surprise.

"I worked for ten years as a telegraph operator for the Associated Press," she said. "I'm faster than Colin. I'd be happy to wire a message."

"Oh, please do!" Rosalind said. "I've never had a chance to see you in action."

The moment he finished breakfast Lucy led him to a small room off the kitchen where a telegraph station had been installed. Mary and Rosalind followed, along with seven-year old Sadie, who was curious about all the activity. Lucy took a seat at the table beside the small Morse sounder, then looked up at him with expectation.

"Do you know the exchange?" she asked.

He opened the small booklet he kept in his breast pocket with the information about the Berlin law office that would be handling the licensing deal. His message wasn't confidential, but there were so many people crammed into this tiny space that it made him tense.

"Please tell them to delay the vacuum contract by one week," he said. His father wasn't going to be happy about the delay, but so long as the contract could be finalized before the end of the year, they could still realize the tax benefits.

"How do you spell vacuum?" Lucy asked.

He spelled it out, and Mary looked at him curiously. "Like those machines to clean a carpet?"

He glanced at her, trying to suppress the smile. "You know that statement is exposing the fact that you haven't read the reports I've been sending you for over a year."

"If those reports involved cleaning carpets, I'm glad I'm not reading them."

He explained how they'd been vacuum sealing their jars since their company began, but he planned to move into canning, and that required an expensive licensing deal with a German inventor for a new type of vacuum seal for cans.

That triggered a whole new round of chatter, with the women bombarding him with questions about what he planned to can and if the food would still taste good. He never liked being the center of attention and wanted to escape to be alone with Mary.

"Could you please send the wire? Tell my lawyer to reschedule the contract signing for the thirty-first of December." He would leave the day after Christmas, spend a few days touring factories in Berlin, another day to meet with his attorney, and then conclude the deal on New Year's Eve. Germans never took that day off. It was one of the things he liked about them.

Lucy must have sensed the impatience in his voice, for she opened the sounder and began tapping out the message. The other women gathered in close to watch, but it seemed anti-climactic, for in less than a minute the rapid tapping came to an end.

"Thank you," he said tersely, then turned to Mary. "When will you be ready to show me the rest of the estate?"

"As soon as I grab my coat. You'll want to bundle up. It snowed again last night."

She was right. At least two inches of powdery white snow had fallen, and the wind blew it into some spectacular drifts. Normally he didn't enjoy the outdoors, especially when an icy chill was snaking down his collar, but it was worth it to be with Mary.

Even though this bittersweet attraction couldn't go anywhere. She would never leave Whitefriars, and he would go stark raving mad if he had to live in this rural isolation. He still enjoyed the way she took so much pride in the barn she was about to show him. He loved that about her. She took such boundless delight in everything from a snowdrift to a newly renovated barn.

The foundation and walls of the barn were mostly of stacked stone, but the top half of the walls and roof were made of wood.

"The barn dates to 1735, and we were able to save most of the original stonework," she said while passing through the wide double door. "My great-grandfather raised the roof ten feet in the 1840s to accommodate the camels he brought back from Africa. One of our less glorious ventures, I'm afraid, for the camels didn't survive."

There were stalls for half a dozen cows and an open pen for the goats. It was warmer in here, but the barn didn't smell too bad. The scent of hay and chilly air masked most of the animal scents. Large tin canisters for collecting milk were stacked near the entrance. She reached over to show him a new cream separator and accidentally knocked over an empty milk can, its clang echoing in the barn.

"Oops! Sorry!" she said as she lifted the cannister back upright.

"Did you just apologize to a milk can?"

"It's a bad habit," she admitted with an abashed smile. "Yes, I sometimes apologize to things, especially if I bump into them or break something. This place is full of old antiques, so I try to be gentle, but sometimes accidents happen."

He would die before admitting it, but he sometimes talked to things, too. "What do you do with the milk?"

"I sell it to a cheesemaker in town. It doesn't earn much, but maybe someday I'll learn to make cheese myself."

He lifted a skeptical brow. "Cheesemaking isn't for the faint of heart," he said. "I'm planning on releasing a brand of Whitefriars gouda cheese in the coming year. I spent most of November in the south of Holland to live with some cheese-makers and learn the process from the ground up."

"You're learning to make cheese?" she said on a bubbly laugh.

He hoped she wasn't about to poke fun, because he'd invested a lot in the cheese idea, and not just money. He enjoyed the process of learning about cheese, everything from its culinary history, the science behind it, the cooking poten-tial, packaging, and preservation methods.

"Yes, there will be a brand of Whitefriars cheese soon," he said. "I'm in the process of buying two dairy farms in upstate New York for it. Six hundred Holstein cows. They're the best cream producers."

They headed outside into the chilly sunshine and began walking toward the eastern fields. He explained how each breed of cow produced different levels of fat content and milk solids. He wouldn't tolerate unreliable results from his milk suppliers, which was why he insisted on owning the cows and manner of production. He inherited his penchant for control from his father. It was their inherent need for control that prompted them to buy this old castle in the first place. Could Mary understand this? He chose his words carefully.

"When our company first began selling apple butter I bought two apple orchards so I could ensure quality. When we began making mustard sauces, I commissioned farms to grow precisely the sort of mustard seed I needed. It was the only way I could guarantee consistency. So now I am acquiring dairy farms."

"I didn't realize you had any interest in making cheese," she said.

He tried not to laugh. "It was all in the reports I've been sending you."

She grabbed a pinecone from the ground and threw it at him.

It hit his shoulder, but he caught it before it dropped to the ground. "Do you want to apologize to this, too? You just treated it shamefully."

She snatched it and threw it against him again, her smile radiant. "Guilty as charged," she admitted.

They walked along the path that skirted the castle and he listened to her wax poetic about the ancient grove of oak trees straight ahead. Rumor had it that a trio of escaping royalist soldiers once took shelter by hiding in the limbs of those trees while Cromwell's soldiers searched the grounds for them. That had been almost three hundred years ago, and while some of the trees were probably long gone, a few of these massive old oaks had witnessed the event.

"We call it the royal oak grove," she said. "I pay an arborist a fortune to keep the trees healthy. Last year one needed to be cut down, and I almost wept as it came crashing down. It had witnessed so much history."

The stump was still there, but less than a yard away a sapling was chest high. She reached out to touch it. "I comfort myself that this little fellow is its offshoot. The older tree was mostly dead and this new one wouldn't have survived if the bigger tree kept stealing all the sun. A hundred years from now it will be alive for our descendants to celebrate and tell the story."

By heaven, she was attractive! How fascinating to see the

world through her eyes. No matter what, he was glad to have come here.

But from the corner of his eye he could see the watermill. Sagging roof, failing stream, and a broken wheel. The Parks had tidied the yard, but it was still a blight on the property. The gardens had gone to seed and there was no lawn to speak of. This sort of squalor couldn't be associated with his line of high-end products.

He turned away to look back at the castle, wishing he didn't have to lay down the law, but he did. There was no easy way to say this, but he tried to speak gently.

"Mary, in bringing paying guests to the estate, you are making a material change to the contract we signed." He pointed to the castle that looked so stately and grand, but surrounding it were goat pens, overgrown gardens, and ram-shackle outbuildings. "That image is on every jar of food I sell. It implies quality and prestige."

Everything about this discussion was intensely difficult, but his corporation was the only thing in the world of which he was truly proud. All his waking hours were devoted to researching food science, tinkering with recipes, investigating advances in packaging and distribution. He loved it all. He had no real friends, no hobbies, and no interests outside of the business he created. This castle was the image of his company, and he couldn't let it be tarnished.

He spoke as gently as he could. "You don't need to lease the rooms. If you need the estate to earn more money, tell me. I can help."

"It isn't the money." Mary's arms were crossed, her look stony.

He couldn't imagine why anyone would want the privacy of their home invaded for any other reason. "Then why?"

She wandered over to sit on the old tree stump, and her lovely smile was gone.

"It gets lonely here," she admitted. "Christmas has always been my favorite season because my family comes. For two weeks a year the castle is filled with laughter and children and conversation. It feels like the way life was intended to be, and I treasure every hour. It's magical, like a perfect world in a glass snow globe. I wish it could be like that the whole year, but it's not."

He understood. He'd die if he had to be trapped out here, in the middle of nowhere with little to do other than renovate a moldering old estate.

"So I'd like to have guests," Mary continued. "They won't be strangers after a few days, and this castle should be shared. I would like to have friends and company. Laughter. Anything except the howling, crushing sense of isolation after every-one leaves."

"If you're that lonely, have you never considered moving into town?"

She slanted him an embarrassed glance. "You saw what happened the last time I went to town."

"The attack of nerves?"

She nodded.

"It always happens?"

"Not always, but I'm never at ease there." She got off the stump and began pacing again, twisting her hands and speaking rapidly. "I don't know why I'm like this, but ever since I was a child I never liked the city. I feel trapped and I can't breathe. I get anxious and can't explain why. My parents wanted to send me away to Paris for an education. That's where they sent Colin, and he loved it, but the thought of being stranded in a big city… no. I can't. Nothing about it appeals."

That clinched it. He would figure out a way to make this work for Mary. They could kill two birds with one stone. He could help her have a magnificent Christmas, and in the meantime, he could help her turn the estate around so it would be suitable for guests.

"The castle lacks a Christmas tree," he pointed out.

Mary winced. "We meant to get one the day Colin discovered your letters. I'm afraid your visit threw us off our game."

"Then let's get the tree today. We've got five days ahead of us, and hopefully by the time I leave, we can have a plan to make the estate ready for visitors."

Her face came alive, and it made him feel ten feet tall. How desperately he wanted to please her, for she seemed to genuinely like him, which was extraordinary. He couldn't imagine why any woman would be interested in a tongue-tied, introverted wet blanket, but he didn't feel like a wet blanket when he was with Mary.

She grabbed his hands, her entire countenance radiating happiness. "Aren't you a constant source of surprise?" she said.

He desperately wanted to kiss her but stopped himself just in time. He couldn't stop the emotions bubbling up inside him.

"Mary, I love being with you. You've got such passion and curiosity. I think if we joined forces, you and I could conquer the world." He stopped, mortified by the emotionalism of what he just said. "I'm sorry—"

"Don't apologize!" She didn't look offended. If anything, she appeared flattered.

"I got carried away. This is rare for me. Unheard of, actually."

Despite the cold, he was awash with heat. If he could melt into oblivion he would welcome it. Once again, Mary knew the perfect thing to say.

"Everett, I feel the same way. You've stormed into my world and alternately thrilled and terrified me, but mostly I'm just happy you're here. Let's go back to the stable and get the sled to carry a Christmas tree home."

***

Mary harnessed the horse and hooked the sled up, because Everett had no experience with such things. He was born and bred for the city. He didn't even have proper boots, only rubber galoshes he pulled over his street shoes.

Maybe that could change. He'd been on the verge of kissing her back in the royal oak grove. She wished he had! She'd wanted to kiss him so badly, but maybe there was another lady in New York. She hadn't forgotten what Colin said about Everett's disastrous engagement that came crashing down a week before the wedding. That was years ago, but perhaps he'd found someone else since, and she desperately wanted to know.

She led the horse out of the stable, Everett walking alongside her. "How is it the ladies of New York have allowed you to remain a bachelor for so long?"

He glanced at her in surprise, his cheeks reddening. It was hard to know if it was from the cold or embarrassment, but he tugged his collar higher as they set off for the woods a few acres away.

"I tend to keep to myself mostly," he said.

"Mostly?"

"I was engaged once. It ended." He didn't sound sad or upset, and after a few more steps he volunteered the details.

"Stella Rowland was a debutante I met at one of my mother's tea parties. Mother was always foisting young ladies on me, and it was altogether awful because I had no idea how to talk to them, but Stella was different. She made conversation easy and seemed to enjoy being with me. We got engaged because I've always liked the idea of having children someday and it was time to settle down. Stella seemed perfectly fine."

Perfectly fine didn't sound like an overwhelming endorsement, but she dared not interrupt. The sled made whispery slicing sounds as it glided over the snow behind them, and she waited for Everett to keep talking, but he seemed sad and awkward again.

"And?" she prompted. Her question dangled uncomfortably, but he eventually started talking again.

"A few days before the wedding everyone started gathering in Manhattan. She had a series of tea parties and such, but I never attended. We planned a one-month honeymoon to Lake Geneva and I was busy at the office clearing my schedule. My father told me I needed to pay more attention to Stella, so I left early one afternoon to surprise her at one of the teas. I overheard her talking to her friends, laughing about me. She was telling them about my etiquette book for gentlemen on how to converse with ladies, because otherwise I was hopeless. They all thought it quite funny."

"But you didn't think it was funny," she said, feeling an ache bloom in her chest at his blank expression.

"No, I didn't," he admitted. "Stella's father was up to his eyeballs in debt, and I suppose that was why she was willing to marry a man who needed an etiquette book to carry on a conversation. After that, I knew it would be impossible to feel at ease around Stella again. I broke the engagement that evening, and it caused quite a scandal. I took all the blame and let her be the aggrieved party. I suppose she was. My father said that it was 'poorly done' on my part, and he was right. I'm glad for it, though. I wouldn't have been able to spend the day with you like this if I had a wife back home."

The snow was deeper now. It took some work to trudge through it and she became breathless, partly from the exertion, but mostly from excitement. Everett had shaken off his momentary gloom. He had nothing but happiness on his face.

"No regrets?" she asked.

With a gloved hand he reached for the horse's bridle to bring it to a stop, then closed the distance between them, his face tender as he regarded her. Then he tipped her chin up and he lowered his face to kiss her.

She stepped closer and his arms closed around her. Nothing ever felt so perfectly right.

"Should I apologize?" he asked when he pulled away.

"Please don't. It would spoil everything."

His eyes twinkled. "Then can I do it again?" He must have read the response in her face, for he smiled and leaned in again. This might possibly be the most romantic moment she'd ever had. The snow, the man, the feeling of contentment mingled with exhilaration.

She started smiling. She couldn't help it, she just felt so happy.

She pulled back a few inches. "I'm glad you're here."

"Who else would help cut down your Christmas tree?"

"Exactly so!" She grabbed the horse's bridle and started walking again. It was colder in the shade of the forest, but they wandered amid the elms, oaks, and spruce trees looking for the perfect tree. They passed plenty, but she wanted to prolong this magical interlude of privacy in the woods. They delayed so long her fingers and toes were becoming frozen, and she finally settled on a blue spruce, only about eight feet tall, that would be perfect in the parlor.

Everett started kicking snow away from the base of the tree while she retrieved the tarp and a crosscut saw. She clutched the handle as she approached, standing only inches away and not yet ready to turn the saw over to Everett. She bit her lip, and he understood.

"Do you want to apologize to the tree?" he asked with teasing affection but no mockery. She smiled in relief, then hunkered down, the pine needles scraping the side of her face as she wiggled in close enough to touch the bark.

"We're sorry about this, little spruce. I hope you will enjoy Christmas with us."

Everett spread the tarp on the ground, knelt, and began sawing at the base of the tree. She held the top, tilting it away as he sawed through the trunk.

It didn't take long, and soon the tree was on the tarp as she and Everett each grasped a corner to haul it out of the woods. Once the tree was on the sled they began walking home while she pointed out sights along the way: the badly scarred tree that had been struck by lightning, the ancient cemetery used by the monks, an old stone that had Viking runes carved on it.

"Vikings?" Everett asked. "That's the first I've heard of Vikings at Whitefriars."

"Oh, those are some of our best stories!" she said. How could she not have told him of the famous legend of Father Michael and Hakon the Viking? Especially given his interest in food? "The battles between the Christians and the Vikings in this part of England were epic. For the most part, the Vikings won. They plundered and pillaged, and monasteries were always their favorite targets because they were rich. Whitefriars took quite a beating, with the Vikings stealing the gold and the sheep, but leaving them with their lives. The Viking warlord was named Hakon, and once his people were established in this part of Yorkshire, there was plenty of resentment among the English. Fires, retaliation, that sort of thing. The monks had a lot of sway over the locals, and Hakon struck a deal with Father Michael of Whitefriars to end the bloodshed. They sealed the deal in the gathering room of the original monastery."

It was hard to keep talking while trudging through the snow and soon she was winded. She caught her breath while smiling up at Everett, who seemed spellbound, urging her to continue.

"It was customary to break bread, but it was Christmastime and all the monks had was a few pans of gingerbread," she said. "Hakon had never tasted anything like it, and legend says he renegotiated the deal on the spot, asking for the monks to deliver gingerbread to his stronghold every year at Christmas to keep the deal alive. The truce lasted until 1066 when the Normans came and changed everything. Still, that truce resulted in three generations of peace between the monks and the Vikings."

"I don't believe it."

"It's true!"

"The Vikings would declare a truce, year after year, all for gingerbread?"

She lifted her chin. "It was probably very *good* gingerbread. And I know it's true because they struck a coin to celebrate the truce. It has a cross on one side, and a longboat on the other. We still have it locked up in my father's old desk."

"You're going to have to show me," he said, excitement on his face.

She grabbed the horse's reins and picked up her pace, slogging as fast as she could through the snow, laughing, joking, and panting. Everett took over the horse so she could move easier, but they were both out of breath by the time they arrived at the castle. She brought the tree all the way up to the front door and dropped the reins.

Mercifully, Colin and Nick had returned from their non-grouse-hunting trip. "The tree is outside the front door," she hollered down the hall to Colin. "Bessie needs to be rubbed down and stabled!"

She wasn't going to do it, she was too eager to show the Viking coin to Everett. After stomping the snow from their shoes, she grabbed Everett's hand to lead him down the hallway to the library. It had always been her favorite room in the castle. With warm oriental carpets covering the floor and a wall of bookshelves, it felt like she could explore the whole wide world from this spot. A massive mahogany desk dominated one end of the room. She tugged off her coat, tossed it over a chair, then grabbed the key to the desk from its hiding spot beneath an old atlas.

Her fingers trembled as she knelt to unlock the drawer. "My father used to take it out every Christmas to set on the table along with a pan of gingerbread. I don't know where the original recipe is, but he swore it's in here somewhere." The lock was tight and it squeaked as she turned the key. She tugged the drawer out and rummaged through the old deeds and papers to find the small leather case holding the coin.

She sat in her father's chair and opened the box. Sunlight illuminated the dull gleam of old gold as she tipped the box to free the coin. It wobbled and rotated before settling into place.

"Good heavens," Everett said as he sat on the arm of the chair to lean down, admiring the cross that had been crudely stamped onto the coin almost a thousand years ago. He traced the edges reverently, then turned it over to see the longboat. He shivered, as though a ripple from the past had just whisked through the room.

"Isn't it amazing?" she whispered.

"Yeah," he said weakly. When he turned to look at her, his face was flushed, eyes bright. He leaned down and kissed her again. The library door was open and they could be caught any moment, but she didn't care.

"Is there really a recipe written down for the gingerbread?" Everett asked when they finally stopped kissing.

"The legend says it was written down. Life could be short, and the monks dared not risk losing the recipe should the baker die, so it was written down on lambskin in Latin. The castle has changed hands so many times over the centuries, so it's probably long lost, but my father was convinced it's still here somewhere."

"We *must* look for it," Everett said.

She laughed. "Why? I have a feeling your gingerbread would be better."

"Not true," he said. "A lot goes into the appeal of a recipe. The food's presentation, the aromas, and if there is anything special about the history or the ingredients, it adds a certain magic that can't be defined." He picked up the coin, holding it before them. "And *this* is quite a story."

She scanned the library with acres of bookshelves, all weighed down with leather-bound tomes and boxes of old records. It would take days to search those shelves, but the recipe could be anywhere on the estate. The castle had two dozen rooms, with caches, attics, and cubbyholes everywhere.

"We could spend weeks turning the estate upside down and still not find it. I don't know if it exists anymore."

He didn't seem discouraged. If anything, it seemed he'd been lit by a jolt of electricity. "I know I sometimes appear stodgy and dull, but I have a tiny ounce of poet in me that would like to believe that the truce between the Viking and the monk was real. That the marauder and the pacifist actually broke bread together. I want that recipe."

If desire alone could make something happen, the buoyant anticipation in Everett's face would find that recipe. She didn't think it existed anymore. The practical side of her warned they would be doomed to disappointment, but he clasped her hands and beamed into her face and she couldn't deny him the chance to start searching.

CHAPTER NINE

EVEN THE FRIGID temperature in the tower room couldn't dampen Everett's excitement as he rose before dawn, took a piping-hot shower, then shivered while waiting for his hair to dry. The problem with a hot shower was that it felt good while using it, but the second he turned the water off he had sopping wet hair and damp skin in the chilly, drafty tower room.

Shaving was a challenge when a smile kept threatening, but today would be an adventure. Finding the gingerbread recipe was a long shot, but he simply wanted to be with Mary. No arguing about tenants or licensing agreements. He'd fallen in love, and this was new, uncharted territory for him.

He hadn't loved Stella Rowland. For a while he thought they would be a solid match, but this feeling was entirely different. When he was with Mary he wanted to conquer the world, climb a mountain, call down the stars. Or perhaps find an old gingerbread recipe.

He wiped the remaining soap from his face, dressed, and bounded toward the main section of the castle, which was foolish, for it was still dark and no one would be up.

Except Mary. A lantern illuminated the kitchen, where she had a kettle heating and was dressed for dirty work.

"Is it going to be that bad?" he asked with a glance at the shabby trousers she wore.

"Most assuredly," she said as she poured him tea. "Over the years I've sorted through attics and rooms that haven't been touched in decades. I hope you aren't overly fond of those trousers, because today will be grubby work."

It didn't matter. He'd buy new clothes if need be, but he was anxious to get started, even if it was still dark. She was too.

They began in the library, all the kerosene lamps turned on high. He climbed a ladder to hand down book after book from the top shelves, searching behind the volumes while Mary fanned the pages. It was hard not to become distracted as she stumbled across old documents, notes written in the margins, even a love letter dated from February of 1823. The ridges on his hands were soon coated with grime, and dust made his nose twitch, but he and Mary talked and laughed the entire time.

Their laughter attracted attention, and as the sun rose, others wandered into the library to peek at the chaos created by stacks of books filling the floorspace. Lucy and Rosalind listened in drop-jawed amazement to the story of the fabled gingerbread recipe, but they didn't last long in the dusty air.

Just as well. Everett no longer felt shy around them, but he wanted Mary to himself. The scent of eggs and bacon soon reached into the library, but he didn't want to leave for something so inconsequential as a meal. Not when he and Mary were on a treasure hunt. Eventually Colin brought them a platter of scrambled eggs and buttered toast late in the morning.

"Are we going to be treated to another culinary feast tonight?" Colin asked when he came to retrieve their plates. "I've been remembering that roasted chicken with great fondness. Perhaps we can even coax that Greek trio to play for us again."

An idea seized him at the mention of the Papadakis brothers. "Let's get them to help look for the recipe," he said. "I'm only here for a few more days, and this is a big job."

"Okay!" Mary readily agreed.

They bundled into their warmest coats and set out for the gatehouse, and she let him hold her hand as they wandered down the path. Holding hands had limited appeal when both parties wore gloves, so as soon as they rounded the bend he pulled her behind a juniper tree for a stolen kiss.

"I probably taste like dust," she said with a sparkle in her eyes.

"I didn't notice. Let's try again."

No, she didn't taste like dust. Everything about this morning tasted of joy and discovery. It was a while before they set off again, and as they passed the inoperable mill he suggested they recruit the Parks to help search for the recipe, too.

"Not a good idea," Mary said as she grabbed his arm, pulling him back toward the drive.

"Why not? They aren't doing the estate any good with making pottery."

"I still don't like to interrupt them without warning."

He looked at her curiously, and her embarrassed expression confirmed his suspicions. The practical side of him was tempted to rant about letting useless tenants take advantage of her generosity, but he was beginning to understand Mary's position regarding her tenants. He traced a gloved finger along the line of her jaw.

"I think I understand why you need the Parks and the brothers. There's something to be said for the warmth of fellowship."

The relief in her eyes was humbling. Had it only been five days ago when he marched onto this estate and wanted to evict her tenants, demolish the outbuildings, and remake the estate to suit his business needs? Never had he been humbled so swiftly or so wonderfully.

This would soon become difficult. His life was in Manhattan, and Mary couldn't even visit the modest city of York without becoming overwhelmed. She could never make a life with him among the millions of people in Manhattan.

But he still had four more days here, and he wouldn't let the shadow of their inevitable separation darken them. Each hour would be savored and enjoyed. And he wanted to find that recipe!

He strode toward the closed door leading into the mill and pounded. "Visitors!" he yelled, laughing at Mary's mortified expression.

Five minutes later he earned the Parks' agreement to search every nook and cranny inside the mill for the medieval recipe, and twenty minutes later he got a similar agreement from the Papadakis brothers.

***

The next two days were the most exuberant of Mary's life. They didn't find the recipe, but she spent countless hours with Everett, wandering the corridors and unrenovated rooms of the castle. While searching the old trunks in the music room he told her about his father and the bets they'd engaged in over the years. Between kisses in the tower attic she told him how she and Colin used to play hide and seek in the outbuildings. Throughout it all she gave thanks for the miracle of finding a man so keenly attuned to her own curiosity and spirit, even though their hours together were dwindling. She could never leave Whitefriars for the bustling world of New York City, but oh, how she would savor these days forever.

They spent most of the morning on the day before Christmas searching the cabinets and drawers in the kitchen for the recipe. They inspected old casks, barrels, crockery jars, and even an old butter churn in the nearby larder. At two o'clock it was time to admit defeat and begin cooking a grand feast for tonight's dinner. They had already agreed today would be their last day to search, for Christmas Day would be devoted to family time.

"I'm sorry we couldn't find the recipe," she said as she set a huge cask back on the shelf. "It would have been wonderful to serve the monk's gingerbread recipe tonight."

Everett smiled. "I loved every moment of searching for it. I guess it doesn't exist anymore."

"Probably not," she said. But the story of the truce between the monk and the Viking was real. The coin proved it, and that tiny piece of metal was the only thing left of the historic agreement. There would be nothing to commemorate her own truce with the American businessman she fell in love with against all odds. Only a bittersweet memory that would die along with her.

It was a depressing thought and she drew a fortifying

breath as she stepped back to smile up at him. "Let's go make the best Christmas Eve dinner this castle has ever seen!"

***

Christmas morning was given over to the children as they opened gifts and gorged on the sweets Mrs. Galloway had prepared. Mary's heart wasn't in it. By midafternoon she escaped with Everett outdoors.

They walked the bumpy stone path along the parapet walls that had long fallen into disuse. Frost covered the stones and she clung to Everett's hand. She'd grown up scrambling over these old stones and didn't need his support, but for a few blessed hours she would savor every moment, for tomorrow he would be gone.

From up here they could see out over the estate, miles of unblemished countryside stripped of leaves and greenery. There was a beauty in the windswept barrenness of the land, but it would be hard for a man of business to live here. Already she could tell he was anxious to move on to Berlin and the contracts he needed to sign. This time tomorrow, he would be nothing but a wonderful memory.

She squeezed Everett's hand as she leaned into the wind, then nearly jumped out of her skin as a trumpet blast shattered the silence.

"What was that?" Everett asked.

A glance down the path showed the Papadakis brothers, Flavian belting out a tune with his coronet. Marco and Theo walked a few paces behind.

"Merry Christmas!" Marco yelled up at them. Hope filled

her chest, for he was carrying something with both hands, held away from his body with care. Everett noticed, too.

"Let's go meet them," he said.

They scurried as quickly as possible over the uneven stones until they reached the staircase snaking down the castle's front wall. They met the brothers at the base. All had broad smiles, and Marco held a scruffy, worn piece of old leather pounded thin and tattered around the edges.

"For you," Marco said, offering the scrap of parchment. Her fingers trembled as she accepted it. Faded black lettering was still visible, written in Latin. She could make no sense of the words, but the document began with a list and then only a few lines of text. The strangest thing was a crude sketch of a Viking longboat at the bottom of the page. This had to be it!

"Where did you find this?" she asked on a shaking breath.

"Bakehouse," Marco said. He started pantomiming with his hands and speaking in Greek but she could make no sense of it.

"Rosalind reads Latin," Everett said. "Let's go."

She nodded, all of them following Everett inside. *Please, please, please let this be the recipe!* It was stained and damaged, the parchment practically falling apart in her hands, but it made sense it would be found in the bakehouse. They should have looked there the first day!

Flavian let out another blast from his trumpet, nearly startling her out of her skin, but it brought the rest of the family hurrying into the great hall. With trembling hands, she set the document on a table near the window.

It looked even worse in the light. The buff-colored parchment was filthy and the lettering cracked with age, but she pulled to the side as Rosalind moved in. It seemed to take forever for Rosalind to slip on a pair of spectacles and lean in close, her face furrowed in concentration.

"My Latin isn't all that it could be," she said hesitantly.

"Is it a recipe?" Everett asked.

Rosalind leaned closer, palms clapped to her face as she scrutinized the document. "I don't understand most of it. But I see the word for honey. And *triticum*. That's Latin for 'wheat.' Yes, I think this is a recipe."

Everett's arms clamped around her and she couldn't breathe. Her feet left the ground as he whirled her around. Everyone started talking and laughing.

"You know this means you're baking tonight," Colin said, but it brought a hearty grin from Everett.

"Just try to stop me," he said with a grin.

They found an old Latin dictionary in the study and Rosalind went to work translating the rest of the recipe. It was seasoned with ginger, cloves, and a dash of black pepper. It called for a shocking amount of honey and used ale for raising the dough.

Everett winced as he studied Rosalind's translation. "As much as I wanted to love this recipe, I don't think it will be palatable to modern tastes. I'll make it anyway... in homage to Father Michael and Hakon the Viking."

Twenty minutes later Mary sat on a stool, grinding cloves into a powder while Everett prepared two batches of gingerbread... one using the monk's recipe and another updated with ordinary yeast and refined flour.

Everett was happier than she'd ever seen him as he whisked honey into the batter. She could happily sit here all day and gape at the way he masterfully chopped ginger with that brisk staccato beat or flicked his wrist while whisking batter in a lightning-fast motion that made him look like a maestro in the kitchen.

"In another life I would have been a cook," he said.

"You're rich," she said. "Why can't you quit and be a cook?"

"Because I'm good at business," he said with a genuine smile. "I could never walk away from Whitefriars Foods. It's a hard and frustrating business, and although sometimes I want to tear my hair out, don't let that fool you. I'm proud of every recipe I created. Every marketing campaign, every improvement to our factory or operations. Sometimes it's the hard things of which we are most proud, and I've sweat bullets over that company."

It didn't look like he minded as he kept working with that faint smile on his face, recounting stories of the deals he worked with his father, their triumphs, and their occasional errors. The look of pride on his face reminded her of the way Colin bragged over his children.

Soon the warm scent of ginger filled the kitchen as the monk's recipe began baking. Everett looked pensive as he measured out ingredients for his version.

"Aside from the rye flour and ale-based yeast, the monk's recipe is wonderfully seasoned," he said.

"Clever monks."

Everett smiled, still surveying the range of ingredients on the counter before him. "It's a creative use of pepper. And the dry ingredients…" He gestured to the cinnamon, nutmeg, cloves, and ginger. "These could be bottled with a touch of dry yeast. I could brand this with the Whitefriars label on the front and the story of the monk and the Viking on the back label. It's too good of a story not to use." He looked up, his eyes meeting hers. "And of course, you'd get a double royalty off the deal. Aside from a little tweaking, you provided the recipe."

She tried to sound stern, but it was hard not to smile. "You Americans. Always thinking of making a profit."

He went back to whisking. "If a monk and a Viking can get along, can't an American and an English lady?"

She sensed a far greater meaning behind his question. This week had been wonderful, but the end was coming fast and she didn't want to face it. Not yet.

"It depends on what you're making for dinner," she said, striving for a lighthearted tone. "You set a high bar for yourself the other night."

He didn't even flinch. "Invite everyone over. Tell the brothers to bring their instruments, and the Parks to keep their hands to themselves. Yes. It's Christmas, and tonight we shall all break bread over a gingerbread recipe a thousand years in the making."

That evening, Colin began the meal by leading them in prayer. "At this holiest time of year, it is right that we remember that God so loved the world that He gave His one and only Son. We give thanks for the miracle of Jesus and the blessings He has bestowed on us all. Tonight, we gather to celebrate that gift. We are drawn from different places and walks of life. We will soon be going our separate ways, but we will always be friends, now and forever."

There was good food, conversation, and music, but it was bittersweet. Across the candlelit table she saw the faint tinge of blue around Sarah's lips. She saw the homesickness in Theo's face. And she felt a pain in her heart knowing that after tomorrow Everett would be gone.

He must have sensed her melancholy thoughts, for beneath the table his hand reached out for hers and squeezed. It was both the happiest and the saddest Christmas of her life, for there would never be another quite like it. The Papadakis brothers alternately played music and indulged in dinner. Everyone sampled from the two pans of gingerbread. The monk's bread was denser and chewier, but oh, what flavor! Everett's was clearly tastier, made with refined flour and beautifully risen. It still engendered plenty of debate as people argued the merits of historical authenticity versus modern improvements. She tried to memorize every moment of conversation, every taunt, every teasing retort. How she would miss this!

Soon the Parks and the brothers bundled up to head home, and the men went to their rooms to begin packing, for they would be leaving early the following morning.

Rosalind lingered to help carry the nearly empty pans of gingerbread back into the kitchen, and she relayed a conversation she'd had with the Papadakis brothers during dinner.

"They're going back to Greece next week," she said. "Theo has had enough of being separated from his fiancée, and since all three of them compose together, they move as a group."

Mary met Everett's gaze, which was tender with sympathy. A week ago he would have said "good riddance," but now he seemed to understand the loss it would be for her.

Rosalind also relayed that she was expecting another child in six months, so they wouldn't be able to come next year for Christmas. It was a double blow. Christmas wouldn't be the same without Nick and Rosalind and their children.

And of course, Everett would be leaving tomorrow, too. He already had his bags packed, and she would wish him the best wherever he went but would not be able to follow.

CHAPTER TEN

ORNING CAME ALL too quickly. Mary met Everett in the kitchen before the others awoke. They bundled up, lit a lantern, then headed outside to the barn, for the goats needed to be milked. Could there be a less romantic way to spend their final hours together? But Everett insisted he wanted to join her.

"I don't want to lose even a moment with you," he'd told her. So here he sat beside her on a milking stool, holding the lantern and teasing her about the way she apologized to the barn door when she bumped into it.

The sun eventually rose, but Mary slowed down her milking, anything to steal a few more moments alone. There were only two more goats left to milk when the barn door opened to reveal Colin standing in the doorway.

"Can I borrow Mary for a moment?" he asked.

Being alone with her frosty older brother was the last thing she wanted. "I have two more goats to milk."

"I can do it," Everett said.

"You're our guest," she protested. "You shouldn't have to milk the goats. I didn't even know you *could*."

He smiled. "I spent two weeks on a dairy farm. I can milk a goat. Go talk to your brother."

She drew a fortifying breath, wishing that Everett couldn't see through her quite so easily. She followed Colin to the royal oak grove.

"Yes?" she asked when she was sure they were in private.

"I came to ask if Lucy and I will be welcome next year for Christmas."

She gasped. "Of course! Why would you think otherwise?"

He merely quirked a brow at her, and she looked away. She'd meant to hurt him with those accusatory words at dinner the other evening. She wished she could be magnanimous enough to smile and say all was well, but the way Colin waltzed off to his new life in America still hurt.

"Mary, I'm sorry," he said, his voice earnest. "I shouldn't have abandoned you. I was out of my mind with love for Lucy, but I knew you'd rise to the occasion here at Whitefriars."

He still didn't seem to understand. "It wasn't easy."

"Great accomplishments seldom are," he said with a curious gleam in his eyes. "And what you've done here is truly great. I always knew you were the right person to look after Whitefriars. We both know I never belonged here. The reason I installed that telegraph machine when I was still a kid was simply to escape."

"I never wanted to escape."

"I know," Colin said. "And I worry about that. I think you've become trapped here."

Even talking about leaving made the steel bands constrict around her chest. "I'm not trapped. I just never craved anything badly enough to leave it." She wished she wasn't so lonely most of the time, but Whitefriars had everything she wanted, with the lone exception of a family.

She gazed back at the barn. Everett was lugging the ten-gallon cannisters out toward the larder. How desperately she wished he could stay. Colin must have read the longing on her face, for he spoke the words she feared.

"He doesn't belong here," he said. "He and his father have a good life in New York. That business can't be picked up and shipped across the ocean, even if he wanted to."

"I know," she said quickly. Tears were threatening and she needed to end this conversation now. She looked at her pocket watch. "My goodness! Time flies. You'll need to gather up your travelling bags."

"Until next year, then?"

She managed a smile. "Until next year.

***

Everett took a quick shower after milking the goats, then dressed and tidied up the tower room. It had proven a comfortable spot after all, and if Mary could hire a good chef he would have no objections to leasing it.

He carried his travelling bag into the great hall, sorry that this was the last time he would take this walk. His overnight stay had turned into a week, but it was time to leave. A million-dollar licensing deal awaited him in Berlin, and it needed to be finalized before the end of the year.

His footsteps echoed on the bare stone walls of the corridor as he walked toward the great hall. How empty the castle seemed. All of Mary's American family had left an hour ago to catch a train to Liverpool, then sail home. That left her alone in this house with only Mrs. Galloway inside and two stable hands outside. He would go stark raving mad trapped here.

He set his bag in the hall and braced his hand on the mantelpiece, bowing his head in prayer. It didn't have to be this way. Maybe he could convince her of another way. He had to at least try, because he was mourning her loss already.

She must have heard him come down, for her footsteps echoed as she approached. Her welcoming smile vanished when she saw his travelling bag. It was like a fist to the chest, but she had to know he would leave. He had to.

"Shall we go for a walk?" he asked. "I don't have to leave for another hour, and I'd like to discuss something."

She nodded. "I'll fetch my cloak."

A few minutes later they were walking down the path as he tried to think of the right words. She might not welcome his suggestion and it was best to ease into it.

"I've thought more about the gingerbread recipe," he said. "It will take a couple of months to fine tune the ingredients and design a label. If all goes well, I can release it in limited markets by May."

May was a good time of year in Manhattan. The trees lining the streets would be leafy and evening festivals in Central Park would have begun. He could show her the city at its best.

"I'd like to plan a major campaign to roll out the gingerbread spice," he said. "A special tin, the kind people will collect as a keepsake. The story on the back. I think we can get press attention."

He waited for her to respond, but she looked pensive as

she walked beside him. This wasn't going well, but it was time to bite the bullet.

"I'd like you to come to New York," he said. "You could help promote the gingerbread. We could host gatherings, serve gingerbread, talk to journalists. Manhattan in springtime can be wonderful, and I would be with you the whole time."

She stopped, turning to gape at him. "Are you insane?" she asked. "You know I can't go to Manhattan."

He swallowed hard. "Have you ever tried?"

"I can't even go twenty miles into York. I couldn't go to London for a season. I couldn't go to Colin's wedding or college on the continent. So no, I can't go to New York."

The swiftness of her rejection hurt. He didn't need a list of all the things she couldn't do; all he needed to know was if she cared enough to fight for him. The invitation to New York wasn't really about promoting the gingerbread, it was only a pretext for getting her there. What he needed to see was if Mary could learn to live there. If there was any future for them, she would need to be able to leave Whitefriars, if not forever, at least part of the year.

"I'll be beside you the whole time," he said. "I'll even come back to England and sail over with you. We can do this together. I know it won't be easy, but the things that are great in life rarely are. It can be frightening to step out into something new. I've been doing it most of my life and it's never been easy. I've been knocked down, but then comes the time to crawl back up onto your feet, start walking, then running, and don't stop until you get where you need to be. Mary, I'm asking you to come to New York."

She turned away, cradling her arms around herself as she walked back toward the castle. He scrambled to catch up.

"It isn't just the gingerbread. I hope you know that. I care for you. Desperately. I don't want this to end here."

"Neither do I," she said, still walking. "And you should know you have an open invitation to stay at Whitefriars as long as you wish. Stay forever, if you like."

He shot an arm out to slow her, turning her shoulders to face him, but she kept her eyes averted, her mouth tense.

"What are you saying?" he prodded.

She glanced up at him. "I don't want this to end, but I can't ever leave this place. I love it too much."

"It's becoming a prison for you."

She shook her head, trying to smile but not quit getting there. "There are so many things I wish for, but most of them begin and end right here. Sometimes I'm lonely. *Most of the time* I'm lonely, but it's home and I can't leave."

"Mary, I'm lonely, too." She looked taken aback, but could she doubt it? He scrambled for words to explain. "Sometimes being in a crowd of people is the loneliest feeling on the planet. I've never felt this kind of connection to someone before. I thought perhaps you felt it, too."

She shivered and turned away. "I do, but I don't see it coming to anything. I'm sorry about that."

He glanced away. Well. That was that, then.

Leaving this place hurt more than anything he'd ever experienced. He'd come here to defend the image on a label of food, and he succeeded. So, a triumph.

But it didn't feel like a triumph. For the rest of his life he would be looking at bottles, jars, and cans printed with the Whitefriars label, the iconic oval etching of the castle forever reminding him of this week.

He swallowed hard and tried to shift his focus back to

business. He was on firmer ground when speaking of practical matters, and there were still details to conclude before he left for the train station.

"I'll hire a crew to commence renovations on the bake-house," he said. "Since it was where the recipe was found, I don't want it torn down. It will be good for publicity. If you want to turn it into an artist's studio, that's fine. If you want to lease the tower room, that will be fine too, but you'll need to hire a real chef. The meals must be at a certain standard, and it's not fair to ask it of Mrs. Galloway. Since I'm making it a requirement, I'll pay for the chef."

She nodded. "That's more than kind. And will you sign an addendum to the contract allowing me permission to lease the tower?"

"Of course. I'll have a lawyer write something up and forward it to you. Or Colin can sign it, if you'd prefer not to hear from me again."

It looked like she was about to cry but he prayed she wouldn't. This week had been too wonderful to end in tears.

"I'll be able to sign," she said with a watery smile. "I'll look forward to it."

He nodded. "Right, then." He provided her with the tele-graph exchange of the hotel where he'd be staying in Berlin, and his Manhattan one, too. He had no idea how long it would take his lawyer to send the paperwork, but he provided her with all his contact information.

What else was there to say? He had a train to catch and a contract to finalize in Berlin. He'd already arranged for a car-riage to drive him to York, and it would be here in ten minutes. He spent those last minutes sitting on the front steps with

Mary, holding her hand and savoring these last moments together. He touched his forehead to hers.

"I'll never forget this week," he said. "You taught me so many things."

"Like what?" she asked.

How could he express having the curtain drawn back and seeing the world through new eyes? He struggled to define exactly how she had changed him, and it took a while to find the words.

"You've taught me an appreciation for the past," he finally said. "All my life I've looked forward. Planning, hoping, and wishing... always looking forward, never back. You taught me to appreciate the value of the past and where we came from. History. Family. The joy of a chilly December day with a beautiful woman by my side."

He held her closer, wishing there was some solution for them, but he couldn't stay here. Mary might draw strength from Whitefriars, but he would wither here. His entire life felt like it was at a turning point. Stay or go; stay or go....

He had to go. His father depended on him. His business and three hundred employees were in New York. And if he stayed here, over time he'd grow to resent being forced to share this wonderful prison with Mary.

The clattering of horses' hooves signaled the arrival of the carriage. He stood, wishing this wasn't the end. Given the desolation on Mary's face, she felt the same.

"I'll say good-bye now," she said. "I'm afraid I won't be able to watch the carriage drive away. Must keep a stiff upper lip and all. And the sight of a carriage driving away feels so terrible."

She kissed him, then turned around and walked into the castle without a backward glance.

CHAPTER ELEVEN

MARY WAS STUNNED at how quickly the Papadakis brothers vacated the gatehouse. Three days after resolving to return to Greece they were gone. She donned her work trousers and an old shirt to clean the gatehouse, determined to find new tenants quickly. Whitefriars always felt a little lonely in the weeks after Christmas, but this year seemed especially desolate and deserted. If she could attract some friendly new tenants, perhaps her life wouldn't be so barren.

"Oh, good heavens," she muttered upon seeing the interior of the gatehouse. She held her breath as she made her way to the windows, yanking up the sash to let some fresh air inside despite the frigid weather. The brothers had made a halfhearted attempt to tidy up, as the blankets had been straightened on the beds and trash mounded in the bin, but it seemed they never learned the purpose of a washrag, for grime and filth had taken root on most of the hard surfaces. She'd need to go back to the castle, lug a bucket of hot, sudsy water back here, and get to work.

It was okay. It would get her mind off things, like how

she'd grown so pitifully weak she couldn't set foot off the estate without risking an attack of nerves. Everett's face as she left him on the front steps would probably haunt her for the rest of her life.

Surely it was better to have loved and lost than never to have known love at all. That's what Tennyson said, and who was she to argue with the great poet? She'd been blessed by an enchanted week with Everett, and even though it hadn't ended well, she would never regret it. She kept reminding herself of it as she scrubbed the blooms of mold from the gatehouse counter and carried the bedding to dump outside on the frost-covered ground. She was tempted to burn it but would ask one of the stable hands to drive the sheets into town for a professional wash and bleaching.

She comforted herself with thoughts of her first hot shower in the tower washroom tonight. She had the run of the entire castle and could take a hot shower twice a day if she wanted. Three times! There were advantages to living alone.

But dinner was hard. Mrs. Galloway had left for a well-deserved visit with her daughter and grandchildren for a week. Mary puttered in the kitchen, wondering if she dared try to replicate any of the meals she watched Everett prepare with such ease. There was an entire shelf brimming with Whitefriars sauces, but she'd never used them before.

She ran her finger along the label on a jar of balsamic caramelized onions. Everett said to serve it with a little goat cheese on toast, and that seemed easy enough. She also made some soup with a few healthy dollops of beef bourguignonne sauce. It was so good she couldn't bear to eat it alone and darted down to the watermill to invite the Parks to join her for dinner.

They brought a bottle of cider and plenty of good cheer. It seemed wasteful to heat the rest of the house, so they ate in the warmth of the kitchen, every lantern flickering and making the room remarkably cozy.

For a while they laughed and gossiped about the assorted guests who were now gone for another year. It was a bittersweet topic, but one of the few things she had in common with the Parks. They were so different. The Parks were passionate, entirely absorbed in one another, and soon they were snuggling and stealing kisses each time her back was turned.

It was a little off-putting, but she could not resent them. Sarah's lips had a blue tinge during Christmas dinner. She was healthy today, which might account for their amorous mood, but it was impossible to tell how long that good health would last.

She set out the last of the gingerbread for dessert. They toasted the new year, and Mary did her best not to weep.

***

That night Mary sat at her father's desk in the library, turning the Viking coin over and over in her palms. That monk who ventured forth to confront the marauders must have been so brave! Frightened, too, but mostly brave. He probably dreaded facing the Vikings, but what choice did he have? The barbarians were at his door. He dealt with it. Figured out a way to survive and soldiered on.

She swallowed hard. Here she sat, safely ensconced behind castle walls that had been built on the very spot where the monks forged a truce with the Vikings. She could stay here the rest of her life, if she wanted.

But she also wanted to be a brave person who was worthy of the Whitefriars name. It would be hard to get on a carriage and go to the city tomorrow, but she could do it. She had a paper bag and Everett taught her how to battle through her panic attacks.

Once she was in York, she could board a train to London.

And then take a ship to Calais.

From there she'd have to find a train to Berlin. How long would all this take? How many times would the terrible fits of panic overtake her on the journey? She should have taken Everett up on his offer to travel with him, but she hadn't. She'd been too cowardly and instinctively rejected it, but something he said on that last day made sense to her.

"It can be frightening to step out into something new. I've been knocked down, but then comes the time to crawl back up onto your feet, start walking, then running, and don't stop until you get where you need to be."

She set the coin flat on the table, admiring the gleaming cross. She would never understand why God had inflicted such an odd condition on her, but it was time to break free of it. Her favorite Bible verse had always been Psalm 56:3. *When I am afraid I put my trust in you.*

And she was very afraid. She'd never travelled off the Whitefriars estate by herself, but with God's help, she would get to Berlin.

***

The train to London had two benches facing each other with a table in between. The spot beside Mary was empty, but across from her a pair of middle-aged businessmen looked gruff and unfriendly. One had a mustache so large it probably kept him warm at night, while the other scowled at a newspaper.

She was in for a nine-hour train ride to London and, given the tickets the men held, she would be with them the entire journey.

"Excuse me," she said. "As we will be sharing this compartment for several hours, I should probably let you know some of my odd habits. I apologize to inanimate objects, smile for no reason, and on occasion I will cover my face with a paper bag and simply breathe for a while. I thought it best to tell you in advance so you won't be alarmed."

The mustached man gave her a hesitant smile but the one reading the newspaper just scowled more. The carriage jerked as the train started moving, and then they were gliding forward, the train station sliding into the distance.

Maybe this wouldn't be so bad after all. Such a smooth ride. But only a few minutes later the train entered a tunnel, plunging the compartment into darkness for several heartbeats, then it emerged into sunlight and was crossing over a bridge. And it was a *long* bridge, steel cables flying past the windows with dreadful speed, and would this awful bridge never end?

She hadn't expected this. Only five minutes into the journey and already the constriction seized her lungs. The heat, the prickling of sweat, the certainty she was trapped and could never get out of this awful moving box.

She closed her eyes and clapped the paper bag over her nose, glancing at the two gentlemen, who both gaped at her in astonishment.

The one with the mustache leaned over. "Are you all right, ma'am? Shall I send for a porter?"

She shook her head but kept the bag plastered over her nose and mouth. It would be okay; all she had to do was remember how soothing Everett had been that day at the Knightsbridge Inn. He was what she was fighting for. He taught her how to handle this. *When I am afraid I put my trust in you.* She was going to make it through this. She repeated the psalm over and over until the tension eased. The paper bag was still clamped in place, but the psalm had helped and after a few minutes she risked lowering the bag, still trembling, still panting.

"I did warn you," she managed to gasp to the mustached man.

"Indeed, you did," he replied kindly.

She pressed a hand over her heart. It was still thudding, but the compartment no longer spun. "I hope it won't happen again, but I make no promises."

The two men looked at each other, then shrugged. The next few days might be full of similar embarrassments, but between her faith, the paper bag, and her need to see Everett, she would get there.

First London, then Calais, then Berlin. And then?

The rest of her life awaited, and she had no idea what it would look like but had faith that it would be good.

CHAPTER TWELVE

EVERETT CHOSE THIS hotel because the restaurant on the ground floor was reputed to be the finest in Berlin, and he studied the menu carefully. If he asked for the black bean soup to be prepared without the sour cream, it could still be considered black. And German *blutwurst* sausages were mostly black, too. He didn't care for them, but they would do.

He placed his order with the waiter. "I'll also have blackberries for dessert, along with some black coffee," he said.

"Very good, sir," the waiter said as he took the menu card.

Black was always the most challenging food day, and when dinner arrived it was an unappetizing sight. Links of black blood sausage curled around the outside of the plate with a cup of black beans in the center. The sight made him completely lose his appetite.

He went back to studying commodity prices in the newspaper, trying to filter out the laughter from the table beside him. It was New Year's Eve and it seemed the entire city had turned out to celebrate in the streets, sing from the balconies, and drink in the all-night taprooms. At the table beside him, a large family of three generations argued the merits of tea versus coffee. That sort of good-hearted conversation reminded him too much of Whitefriars, and he wasn't quite ready to touch that memory yet.

He raised the newspaper higher, surprised by the falling price of sugar on the Chicago Mercantile Exchange. Perhaps he should purchase a larger order to take advantage—

"Is it a black food day?"

He looked around in disbelief, for Mary Beckwith stood three feet behind him. He shot to his feet. "How did you get here?" he asked in amazement.

"You gave me the address of your hotel before you left."

Of course… the lawyer. The contracts. He shouldn't read too much into her sudden appearance, for she desperately wanted to get that tower room rented. Surely she knew he wouldn't trounce on her if she began leasing it before the contracts had been modified.

He swallowed hard. "You're here about the contracts?" he asked.

Her brows rose, chin lifted on that swan-like neck. She was the most beautiful creature he'd ever seen.

"No," she said simply.

He lowered his head and looked away. *Please.* Please let this be true. When he looked up again, Mary hadn't moved and gazed at him with her heart in her eyes.

"Would you care to join me?" he asked.

A bit of her composure faltered. Was it possible she was as terrified as he? When she nodded he held the chair out for her. She bumped the table when adjusting her seat and apologized to the water glass as she stopped it from wobbling.

He sat opposite her, still not believing his eyes. "Mary, I

didn't think I'd ever see you again. How on earth did you get here?"

"The same as anyone else, I suppose. Train. Boat. Carriage. I needed to prove I wasn't a prisoner of Whitefriars. That I could leave."

He covered her hand with his own. She was trembling, and her sacrifice in coming after him was humbling. It had cost her to come. "And how was the journey?"

"Two attacks of panic on the train to London. None on the ferry to Calais, but six after arriving in France and one about ten minutes ago. And I survived every one of them."

His heart swelled because he knew how hard this journey had been for her. "Mary, I'm so proud of you."

She looked surprised. "I'm a nervous and jittery misfit."

A smile broke across his face. "And I have a plate of black food on New Year's Eve. Which of us is the bigger misfit?"

She glanced down at his plate. "I hope I'm not required to partake in the blood sausage."

"They're having ham with a currant-cherry sauce at the neighboring table and it smells so good I've been going out of my mind."

"Let's order some for us both," she said conspiratorially, and he gladly handed the plate of *blutwurst* back to the waiter. He wasn't sure why she was here, but the fact that she travelled more than a thousand miles meant the world to him.

It also meant he needed to be willing to meet her partway as well.

New Year's revelry made it too loud to carry on an intimate conversation in the restaurant, so after they finished dinner they meandered slowly as he walked her to the inn where she was staying a few blocks away. Snow had begun falling, the fat snowflakes looking soft as they floated down in the gaslit street. Revelers were out, singing carols and shouting well-wishes, but he ignored them as he focused on the woman beside him as she recounted her journey.

"I was scared half the time, but it was an adventure, too." She glanced around the street, admiring the trolleys, the lights strung from the trees, the people carousing on the balconies. "I've never seen anything like this. It's all a little overwhelming, and I'm sorry I've missed so much. Whitefriars will always be home for me, but I need to be as brave and worthy as the people who made the estate survive all these centuries. And I'd like to see New York. I'd like to meet your father and visit Colin in his own home."

Hope bloomed in his chest. If she could live in New York, even if only a few months each year, he would be willing to meet her halfway.

All of this was going too fast. Logic said he should slow down. He turned and offered his arm, continuing their walk down the snowy avenue. "Have you hired a chef yet?"

"I left two days after you. I didn't have time to interview chefs."

"Good."

She looked at him quizzically. "Why is that good?"

He slanted her a knowing look, battling the smile tugging at the corners of his mouth. "I like to keep the options open. Who knows how life will unfold in the coming months? And you know I love to cook."

He should stop talking before he spilled the bottled-up hope and frustrated longing that had been simmering inside. But he couldn't. He loved her too much to be stingy with his feelings, especially given the sacrifices she'd made to be with him tonight.

"I love to cook, and I love being able to share my recipes with the world." He turned to face her. "And I love you. I think I started falling in love even before we met, for your letters were always so filled with so much hope and curiosity. From the moment we met you've been warm and wonderful, even when I was too aloof to return it. Thank you for sharing Whitefriars with me."

She stood on tiptoe to kiss him, and he held her tightly. A few passersby hooted, but he didn't care. They would find a way forward, and tomorrow was the start of a new year and a new life for them both.

CHAPTER THIRTEEN

ONE YEAR LATER
CHRISTMAS EVE

MARY HELD HER breath as she entered the newly renovated bakehouse, a little dismayed at the mess her new tenants had made of the place. Yesterday she'd asked them to straighten up, but artists were rarely known for rabid attention to tidiness. With its original stone walls and new French doors, the space was flooded with light but littered with half-stretched canvases, wads of modeling clay, and a couple of broken easels. Everett would be arriving at Whitefriars this afternoon, and it was important for his first impression of the new bakehouse to be a good one.

"Merry Christmas!" she said to the Dumonts, sneaking over to peek at Alma's canvas. While Mary adored Alma's landscapes, her husband, Jack, was a sculptor and his oddly shaped female figures were a little harder to admire. He insisted on shaping the modeling clay while blindfolded, which gave his sculptures a weird shape that wasn't to her taste, but Jack swore they would sell someday.

"My husband will be here in a few hours," she said with a pointed look at the messy studio. The drop cloths hadn't fully protected the new tile floor, and spatters of paint were painfully obvious. "Now would be a good time to tidy up. He's so fond of the bakehouse because it is where we found that old gingerbread recipe. I promised him it would be well looked after."

"Yes, yes, we promised to get it done," Jack said, still blindfolded as he pinched off another lump of clay. She had been back at Whitefriars for a week and had asked them to clean up twice, but still the paint splotches were on the floor.

"I'm heading down to see Socrates, but I will be back in an hour. Will that be enough time to get the paint off the tiles?"

She was getting better about being assertive. She didn't care if the bakehouse was messy, but Everett did, and she would respect his wishes. Managing the bakehouse restoration from New York had been a challenge, but Socrates was on site and oversaw most of the construction. He was overseeing the new landscaping on the estate, too.

It gave him something to occupy his mind after Sarah died in July. She was buried in the estate's cemetery, and he tended her grave daily. Tonight they would dine on pottery featuring Sarah's forget-me-not design, and the spirit of her artistry would forever be a part of Whitefriars history.

Plans for renovating the watermill had been abandoned. The history of Whitefriars was one of transformation, and instead of milling wheat, the estate had now become a place for artists to live and develop their God-given talent. Socrates still created pottery, and the Papadakis brothers were back and making music again. Theo's new bride came with them from Greece, and they were all gainfully employed. With the castle now leasing the tower room, the brothers drove the guests to town, helped with laundry, and kept the grounds tended in exchange for free rent.

The double doors to the mill were wide open, for all three brothers and Theo's bride were visiting with Socrates.

"Maria!" Theo bellowed, shooting to his feet and holding his arms wide when he saw her. He no longer pretended not to speak English, but she loved that he still called her Maria. Marco, on the other hand, had an entirely different name for her.

"How is Persephone?" he asked as she stepped into the warmth of the mill.

It was a nod to the arrangement she and Everett had splitting their year between New York and Whitefriars, for Persephone was the Greek goddess who lived part of her year above ground and part in the underworld.

For eight months out of the year she and Everett lived in New York, but they would spend two months every summer and two months at Christmas in England. They'd arrived for Christmas last week, but Everett needed to spend his first few days in London on business. She was counting down the hours until his arrival in time for dinner tonight.

"I am surviving New York City very well," she said to Marco.

Although at first it had been dreadful. Their wedding wasn't until April, so for the first three months she lived with Colin and Lucy in the heart of Manhattan where the noise never stopped. Automobile motors, vendors shouting their wares, clopping horses, rattling streetcars, and blaring horns.

The streetlamps remained on all night, so it was never actually dark, and Mary feared she would never adjust to the noisy, chaotic world.

Then she discovered a wonderful thing called a "hot dog." She had been with Lucy after a long day of wedding preparations and they'd been so hungry they didn't want to go into a restaurant to order. A loud vendor was hawking hot dogs from his cart only a yard away. It smelled sinfully good and they gave in to temptation.

Her world was never the same. Mary began venturing out alone for a daily hot dog at lunchtime. She worked up the courage to branch out to sample from different hot dog carts and even ventured in to some of the city's famous delicatessens. It was during these daily forays seeking out hot dog vendors that she started to love New York. The people, the energy, the new adventure on every block. She always carried a paper bag in her purse, and knowing it was there was usually all the comfort she needed to hold back looming panic.

She was admiring a new collection of pitchers Socrates had just taken from the kiln when a familiar voice made her heart thrill. "Anyone home?"

It was Everett, looking windblown and delightful as he stood in the open doorway. She raced across the mill and into his arms, ignoring the others as she indulged in a long, welcoming kiss.

"How was London?" she asked.

"Busy. Profitable. How's the bakehouse?"

Mary winced. It had been only twenty minutes since she'd seen it, and she doubted the Dumonts made much progress, and Everett's standards were terribly high.

"Why don't you join us in a hot toddy?" she said. "I'm not sure the bakehouse will be up to snuff yet."

Marco began preparing the hot toddy while Socrates slipped out to warn the Dumonts. Everett took the mug but noticed exactly what was going on.

"What's wrong with the bakehouse?" he asked.

"Nothing's wrong," she stressed. "But artists, you know…"

"Actually, I don't know," he said. "What's wrong with the bakehouse?"

Last year he wanted to tear the bakehouse down, but now it occupied a huge part of his sentimental heart because of that gingerbread recipe. He'd come to appreciate the history of this place as much as she, and his gingerbread idea was selling marvelously in New York.

"Don't worry," she assured him. "The bakehouse has survived far greater trauma than some paint spatter and a pair of messy artisans. Give Socrates a few minutes to tidy up, then you can go see the wonderful transformation that's taking place over there."

And tonight she and all their tenants would have a feast in the great hall. They would dine on food seasoned by a creative American genius, served on platters featuring Sarah's forget-me-not design, and share a gingerbread recipe a thousand years in the making. She fought hard to rescue Whitefriars from the ravages of time, and in so doing became strong enough to leave it.

Whitefriars would continue to grow and change with the passing of the generations, and she had now earned a place in the history of this wonderful castle.

The End

If you enjoyed *Christmas at Whitefriars*, you may enjoy the earlier books in the series!

A DANGEROUS LEGACY

Telegraph operator Lucy Drake is a master of Morse code and has made herself a valuable asset to the Associated Press news agency. But the sudden arrival of Sir Colin Beckwith at rival British news agency Reuters puts her hard-earned livelihood at risk. Colin is talented, handsome, insufferably charming—and keeping a secret that jeopardizes his reputation. Colin is on a quest to save his ancestral estate of Whitefriars, but his alliance with Lucy threatens all he holds dear.

A DARING VENTURE

Dr. Rosalind Werner is at the forefront of a ground-breaking new water technology, but she needs the government to endorse her work. Nickolas Drake, Commissioner of Water for New York, is skeptical—and surprised by his reaction to Rosalind. While they fight against their own attraction, they stand on opposite sides of a battle that will impact thousands of lives and the future of New York City.

ABOUT THE AUTHOR

Elizabeth Camden is best known for her historical novels set in gilded age America featuring clever heroines and richly layered storylines. Before she was a writer, she was an academic librarian at some of the largest and smallest college libraries in America, but her favorite is the continually growing library in her own home. She lives in Florida with her husband who graciously tolerates her intimidating stockpile of books.

Made in the USA
Las Vegas, NV
19 April 2021

21674269R00090